TEXAS JUSTICE

"You want to take the three of us?" the marshal said to Garrity. "You think you're that good, do you?"

Durkin cut in, saying, "It won't be just Garrity. You got to take me into account."

Garrity figured to kill the marshal if it came to killing. He wondered how fast Durkin was with a gun, because the deputies looked as if they might be fast enough.

"You were about to kill an unarmed man, Marshal," Garrity said. "Couldn't let you do that."

The marshal just stared at Garrity.

"What do you want, Marshal?" Garrity said. "You want a shootout or you want to do your job?"

JACK SLADE
TEXAS RENEGADE

LEISURE BOOKS　　**NEW YORK CITY**

A LEISURE BOOK®

September 1993

Published by

Dorchester Publishing Co., Inc.
276 Fifth Avenue
New York, NY 10001

Printed in the United States of America.

Chapter One

It was the first time Garrity had seen long-necked bottles of McSorley's Cream Ale in a silver champagne bucket. It stood on the colonel's desk with two tall glass mugs beside it. He knew it had to be for him since the colonel seldom drank anything but brandy and champagne. The colonel was very genial that morning and Garrity wondered what the old rascal was up to.

"Come in, come in, my dear fellow," the colonel said as he unlocked the steel door of his second-floor office in the Maxim Arms Company warehouse on Crosby Street on New York's Lower East Side. "Sit down while I pour you a mug of McSorley's finest. Old Mac may be six feet under the shamrocks, but his family keeps up the tradition."

Col. Pritchett poured carefully so as not to get too much head on the smooth ale Garrity liked so much. Then he poured one for himself and sat down behind his desk. "Your good health, sir," the colonel said and buried his mustache in the foam.

Garrity emptied his mug and set it down on the desk. He was thirsty and it was good ale, maybe the best in the world. "I know it's not St. Patrick's Day," he said.

"Ha. Ha." The colonel barked his parade-ground laugh. He was tall and thin and 60 or so, with a cropped white head, a leathery face and grizzled mustache. One of his eyes was covered by an eye patch, the other twinkled merrily. "Must it be a special occasion for two good fellas to share a brimming beaker?"

He's sending me to my death, Garrity decided. It wasn't a special occasion, but the assignment he was going to get had to be. It was the first time the colonel had sent out for ale. So he was suspicious and maybe it showed, more so when the colonel opened another bottle.

"Have you ever heard of Alexander Kinnock? Lord Kinnock?" the colonel asked. "Of course, you haven't, but you're going to make his acquaintance. Lord Kinnock is a young Scotsman who recently bought a vast ranch and built a meat-packing plant in Lawton, Texas. West Texas. The Panhandle. He made a huge investment and by all accounts a successful one until he began having trouble with the local Ku Klux Klan, a scurrilous bunch, and an equally thuggish labor organization that calls itself the United Workers of America. You don't seem too surprised?"

Garrity drank his second mug of ale right to the bottom. "I'm more surprised by the UWOA than the Klan. The Klan is always lurking in the bushes, but it hasn't had much success lately. The Army put the fear of God into them back in the Seventies. I thought they were all washed up. But what the hell is the UWOA doing in West Texas? There's nothing there to organize."

"They've got Kinnock's packing plant to organize. It's a big plant, employs a lot of men, and they mean to get their grubby hands on it. However, at the moment the Klan is the more serious threat. Cattle have been stolen from the holding pens at the plant. Hundreds of cattle in night raids. Kinnock's men have been beaten and bullied. Essential machinery within the plant has been damaged. Do you get the picture?"

"Not yet. Why would the Klan want to make trouble for a man who provides so many jobs? There's a depression on and West Texas is dirt poor even at the best of times. Is it extortion?"

Col. Pritchett drank some ale and wiped his mustache. "No, it's not extortion. The Klan wants to drive Kinnock out because he's hired a lot of blacks and is paying them wages equal to those of his white workers. Worse than that from the Klan's point of view, he makes them work together, side by side as it were, and he treats his blacks as fairly as his whites. Better than his whites, the Klansmen say. He's built them a school and hired a teacher. It's open to whites as well as blacks, but as you can imagine, no white man would be caught dead in the place. Actually, I can't blame them. But this racial thing is just an excuse."

It was obvious that the colonel disapproved of Kinnock's experiment. He hated colored people of all races and even those that he didn't hate outright he found offensive. His ingrained bigotry was developed during 30 years service in the British Army, most of it spent in India, Burma and the Sudan. It hardened even more when he was kicked out of the army for ordering his men to shoot down 200 unarmed prisoners during the last months of the Second Afghan War of 1878-1880. Out of the army, without a pension, he had gone to work for the Hiram Maxim Arms Company. Ten years later he was head of the Maxim Company in North America.

Col. Pritchett went on. "The man behind the revival of the Lawton County Klan is a villain called Lamar "Pig Meat" Mayfield." The colonel placed his hand on a buff-colored folder. "It's all in the Pinkerton report. They sent an agent there at my request. You can read it later. Mayfield is a former congressman who controls the Democrat organization in Lawton County, which is a very big county. He controls the present congressman, Riley Turnbull, as well as all political jobs from cow-tick inspector to circuit judge. You can't get a state or county job in Lawton County unless you're a true-blue Democrat and have Mayfield's blessing. He gets his nickname because of his great fondness for pork. It's said he'd rather eat pork chops than choice porterhouse."

The colonel paused to drink and Garrity said, "Mayfield wants to drive Kinnock out, make him sell cheap?"

"That's the size of it," the colonel said. "Mayfield is greedy as well as gluttonous and miserly. He's a wealthy man with a fine big ranch, but that's not enough for him. He covets what Kinnock has and means to get it one way or another. Miserliness and greed go hand in hand. He drinks the cheapest rot-gut and never buys a drink unless he gets something out of it. He wears the same suit year in and year out and has his shoes soled and heeled until they fall apart. He does give his men off the Fourth of July and Christmas Day, but if they want turkey instead of stew, they have to buy it themselves."

Garrity had heard enough about Mayfield's cheapness. "How dangerous is he?"

"As dangerous as can be. Mayfield has a bad history going back at least twenty years. He started small and worked his way up to his present position by all manner of villainy, and that includes murder. I'm sure he's never killed anyone personally, but he's had it done. A number of small ranchers who refused his ridiculously low bids simply disappeared. Their heirs, in most cases, were more sensible. Mayfield has a law degree, but has never practiced for reasons of his own. Not enough money in it, probably. But he does know the law and he knows how to twist it. So he exercises his power in different ways. Everybody he puts into a job has to return part of his salary to Mayfield, even Congressman Turnbull, it's said. Why not? Turnbull serves at Mayfield's pleasure and not the voters. Mayfield can turn him out of office at the next election and he knows it. Kinnock has found himself a real enemy in that dreadful man."

Garrity helped himself to the last bottle of ale. "What about these UWOA organizers? They can't get along too well with the Klan."

"They're making more trouble for Kinnock than they are for the Klan. So far they haven't tangled, but it has to come to bloodshed. Up till now the Klan has steered clear of them because they're all tough fellas who have been through the labor wars in the Northwest. Copper mines, coal mines, lumber camps, railroad strikes. There are twelve of them and a ferocious blackguard called Durkin is their leader. Durkin has been threatening Kinnock with what he calls labor action if he doesn't throw his

9

plant and ranch open to the union organizers."

"Durkin wants to organize ranch hands? That's never been done, never been tried as far as I know."

"Durkin means to do it," the colonel said. "It seems farfetched because from what I know of cowboys they move from job to job, never staying long in one place. The Pinkerton agent suspects extortion is the real reason for Kinnock's trouble with Durkin. Durkin hasn't bothered Mayfield so it may well be that he's in cahoots with him. Mayfield may think the more trouble he can make for Kinnock, the sooner he'll get fed up or frightened and sell out at a loss. But there's no proof of Durkin's involvement with Mayfield. He may plan to go after Mayfield once he beats down Kinnock."

Garrity didn't know all that much about the United Workers of America. He'd been in San Francisco during a bloody streetcar strike several years earlier. He'd read about other violent doings, bombings and assassinations in various parts of the West, mostly in the Northwestern states. The business bosses had their thugs; the labor bosses had theirs.

"Did the Pinkertons look into Durkin's background?" Garrity asked. "Is he a crook? Does he have money stashed away?" It was hard to hide anything from the Pinks.

"They dug deep and found nothing. It seems the man's only possessions are the clothes on his back and a few books. If he has anything that might be called a permanent residence, it's a rooming house in Seattle. He's kept his room through thick and thin, sends his rent by mail."

"That sort of rules out extortion."

"Not necessarily. This may be his first go at it. He's forty-two and perhaps he's tired of being poor.

Sometimes men turn crook when they see the shadows growing long and their days short. Mayfield may have promised him a big chunk of money and is holding it for him. Payment on delivery, so to speak."

"Could be," Garrity said. "You still haven't told me how Maxim got into this. Did Kinnock come up with the whole investment himself? Or is Maxim one of his backers?"

The colonel began to scrape his foul-smelling pipe with the tiny silver knife attached to his watch chain. Scraping the bowl of the pipe was the beginning of the ritual Garrity had witnessed many times, always with dread. Soon the fairly small room would be filled with blue-gray smoke that stung the eyes and made it hard to breathe. The electric fan did its best to suck some of it away, but the colonel always managed to keep ahead of the fan.

"Mr. Maxim is one of Kinnock's backers, but not the biggest. Big enough, however. Kinnock could have managed fairly well using his own money, which is considerable, but for a modest man he likes to do things in a big way. He doubled the stock on the ranch and built a completely modern packing plant from the ground up. It's equipped with the latest machinery, conveyor belts, et cetera, and it must have cost a bundle. Then there was his share in the spur line. The railroad refused to bear all the expense. In order to do all that he had to take in outside investors."

"I'm surprised that Maxim would want to invest in the meat-packing business," Garrity said. "A lot of rich Britishers went broke back in the Seventies and early Eighties. Look what happened to that Frenchman who went bust trying to start a meat

11

plant in the Dakotas. They say he lost a couple of million."

"And so he did," the colonel said. "I take it you're referring to the Marquis de Mores. A very wealthy man, to be sure, but it was his extravagance that did him in. For example, there really was no need to build a genuine stone castle in the wilderness. No need for all those liveried servants, no need for all the fancy dress balls, the caviar, the French champagne. Apart from that he made two great mistakes. He paid his workers starvation wages, and they hated him for it, and he hired an incompetent crook to manage the plant. When he woke up one morning and found himself broke, the manager ran off with that week's payroll and the workers burned the plant to the ground."

"I wonder what he's doing now. Head waitering here in New York?"

The colonel was not amused. "Mr. Maxim was well aware of the Marquis's many mistakes, his poor business sense, his callous treatment of his workers. Kinnock is nothing like that. He lives frugally in a large but sensible ranch house. No castles or imported bubbly for him."

"Does he at least take a drink?" Kinnock was beginning to sound too good to be true. Garrity didn't like to work with men who seemed to have no flaws in their character. All too often they had as many cracks in them as cheap restaurant plates.

The colonel said irritably, "He drinks in moderation, if you really must know. Where in blazes was I? Oh, yes. Mr. Maxim knew Kinnock was a sound man when he made his investment. But there's something else I must tell you. Kinnock is related to the Queen through his mother, and he has been invited to stay at Balmoral, Victoria's Scottish residence, on

12

a number of occasions. In fact, Kinnock is one of her favorites."

"And the Queen put pressure on Maxim?"

"That's correct, but I'll wager she didn't put up any of her own money, the old bitch." Because he came from the lower branches of a noble family tree, word of Col. Pritchett's dismissal reached Victoria, and she was supposed to have said, "Pritchett is a brutal blackguard and has no place in *my* lovely army. My brown children must not be treated in such beastly fashion." Or so the colonel claimed, though Garrity sort of doubted it. Anyway, the colonel hated the Queen and all her works and pomps.

The colonel puffed savagely on his pipe. Any mention of the Queen always got him worked up. "Poor Mr. Maxim. I can just hear her saying to him, 'Hiram, I be varry gradeful if you vass to inwest some of your gelt in Kinnock's liddle moo-cow bidness.'"

Garrity didn't think the colonel's German accent was very good.

The colonel laughed, pleased with his impersonation. "She really does talk like that, you know, and I'm quite sure she said something like it to Mr. Maxim. Well, you see, a suggestion like that, coming from old lard face herself, what choice did he have?"

"No more tea at Buckingham Palace if he said no. He'd never get to be Sir Hiram when he finally decides to change his nationality. Sir Hiram-to-be knows how to kiss ass."

"It would take more than a knighthood to get me to kiss that old bitch's ass." Then remembering that Maxim was his bread and butter, the colonel said sternly, "Mr. Maxim kisses no one's arse. However, it's quite possible that he may decide to become a British subject at some stage of the game. There's

here next will note 6:3

been talk of it. After all, he had to go to England to find financial backing for his inventions. He offered his machine gun to the War Department here and they turned him down flat. Now his machine gun, his smokeless powder and other inventions have revolutionized the British Army."

"What does Maxim want us—me—to do?" Garrity asked. "Come to think of it, how did he find out Kinnock was in trouble?"

"Somehow or other, Mr. Maxim manages to keep an eye on all his investments. Suffice it to say he knows something about Kinnock's problems and has directed me to resolve them. He didn't say if possible because to him all things are possible."

"Good for Hiram," Garrity said. "It must be great to be so sure of everything."

The colonel gave Garrity the stern look that was always followed by a warning. "You must handle this matter with the utmost delicacy, involving, as it does, the Queen herself. But more important to me, it has Mr. Maxim's special interest. Should you fail or, heaven forbid, Kinnock is badly wounded or killed, it could result in serious problems for Mr. Maxim. In turn, it would mean problems for me—and you. No more fifty-thousand-dollar assignments, I'm afraid."

So that was what the chilled ale was all about, Garrity thought. The old bastard felt threatened, was between a rock and a hard place, and was counting on Garrity to make things right. But that was all right: everybody acted out of self-interest. With the colonel gone, like as not there would be no more money for the Zunis, the peaceful New Mexico Indians who had raised him as one of their own after his father and mother were killed by Apaches. He gave them most of the money the Maxim Company

14

paid him, but it was never enough.

"Will Kinnock be hard to get on with?" he asked.

"I really don't know," the colonel said. "He's more of a stiff neck than a stuffed shirt, if you get my meaning. I met him just once, so I can't say I know him. He's modest and unassuming for someone so rich. For instance, he insists that everyone call him Kinnock. No misters or my lords, just plain Kinnock. So that's what they call him in Lawton, everybody from the town drunk to the town council, the usual collection of merchants. The impression I got from our brief meeting was that of a terribly stubborn man. Mild mannered men are often the most stubborn because they refuse to argue with you."

Garrity wondered if the colonel had any more ale stashed away. Probably not. "Does he have any guts, Colonel?"

"I don't doubt that he has," the colonel said. "He comes of a fine military family and has seen service himself as a junior officer."

"But will he fight?"

"I'm sure he will if he sees the need of it."

"But so far he hasn't, even with the Klan and the union breathing down his neck? What does it take to make him fighting mad, a red-hot iron shoved up his ass? He's not a Quaker, is he?"

"I expect he's a Presbyterian if he's anything. Look here, Garrity, you'll just have to go Texas and find out what he's like."

"Just as long as he doesn't wear a kilt."

The colonel sighed. "The only time he wears a kilt is on St. Andrew's Day. Andrew is the patron saint of Scotland. Most of his plant workers get the day off and there's beer and barbecue out at the ranch. And now I'd like to show you the weapons you are going to test."

That was more like it. Garrity liked weapons and so did the colonel. It was about the only thing they had in common. On every assignment, Garrity tested one or two of the latest weapons developed or distributed by the Maxim Company. He tested them on human targets—the evil bastards he was sent out to kill and whose deaths benefited everyone.

The colonel unlocked the thick steel door that led to the firing range. To get there they had to pass row after row of racked weapons. Garrity loved the sharp smell of gun oil. The firing range was half a block long and there were thick pine boards and man-sized targets at the far end of it. Only small arms were fired there. Heavier weapons were tested at the Maxim Company proving grounds in New Jersey. Col. Pritchett turned a switch and overhead lights flooded the area with a white glare.

"What the hell is that?" Garrity asked.

"That, my good man, is the Frederick R. Simms's Motor Scout, a military vehicle so new that few people know about it. Mr. Simms is Mr. Maxim's top engineer and planner, so it bears his name. Walk around it, get the feel of the thing. You'll be testing it in Texas."

To Garrity it looked like nothing more than a steel box on four hard-rubber tires. A steel box with a Maxim .303-caliber machine gun projecting through a wide slit in the front. Above the slit was a bullet-proof window. Garrity pushed down the long handle that opened the single door and saw that it was a one-man vehicle. One man drove the Scout Car and operated the machine gun, which was the same model as his own light gun, but without the modifications. The Scout had a single leather-covered seat and it was foot controlled. It was steered by a straight steel bar with curved ends.

"Get in," the colonel urged. "I know you're going to like it. See, the one-and-a-half horsepower gasoline engine is in the rear so the driver doesn't feel the heat. The speed of the vehicle blows the engine heat out through vents in the back. Get in, man."

Garrity got in and closed the door. It was something like being in a steel box, but it was roomy enough for one man. The idea was to steer the Motor Scout with one hand and fire the machine gun with the other. Like his own light gun the Scout machine gun had a pistol grip and a trigger and relied on the thickness of the barrel rather than a water jacket to keep it from overheating. The gun, mounted on an angled steel rod, could be swung this way and that. He shot up some imaginary targets and got out.

"Isn't it a whiz?" the colonel said like a proud father showing off his firstborn.

"It'll take some getting used to," Garrity said. "It's nothing like that armored car we used in Mexico."

The colonel patted the steel roof of the Motor Scout. "Of course it isn't. It's light and fast and completely maneuverable."

"How fast does it go?"

"It has a maximum speed of twenty-five miles an hour. That's over fairly level ground, of course. Think of it, man! Put yourself in the place of a bunch of horsemen and suddenly here's this *thing* bearing down at twenty-five miles an hour, its machine gun chattering. Wouldn't you turn tail and run, that is, if you weren't already riddled by bullets?"

"I think I'd run."

"That's because you're smart. Men not so smart might think it possible to stop the Motor Scout with bullets. Well, sir, ordinary rifle and pistol bullets have no effect on Mr. Simms's creation. It won't stand up to anything heavier than that, nor is it

17

intended to. Want to take a few shots at it?"

Garrity said yes and they moved far back from the Motor Scout. The colonel picked up a loaded Winchester rifle and handed it to Garrity. "Blaze away, old man."

It was a 15-shot Winchester and Garrity fired until the rifle ran out of bullets. The side of the Motor Scout was dented and scratched when he walked forward to take a look, but none of the bullets had penetrated the thin but tough steel plating.

The colonel was delighted. "Want to try it again with a military rifle? That's been done, of course, but you may want to try it."

"No need to." He handed the Winchester to the colonel. "I don't figure I'll be facing military rifles in Texas. How will you ship this thing?"

"Just as it is, in one huge crate. It's remarkably light. Of course the gun will have to be unbolted and stored inside the body. It can be bolted back in place in a few minutes. Other, smaller crates will contain gasoline and ammunition belts. You'll get the hang of it in no time. Now I'll show you the engine. It has a crank handle and its speed is regulated by a pedal on the floor. Come on, I'll show you."

Garrity nodded after he was shown the pedal and the brake, a steel rod set in the floor to the left of the steering bar. Directed by the colonel, he cranked the motor to life, then climbed into the Scout and drove it around the firing range at slow speed.

"Any questions?" the colonel said when he got out.

"What else will I be testing?"

"The grenades I wrote you about. Was there something in my instructions you didn't understand? I thought I went into great detail. They're in those boxes over there"—the colonel pointed—"but I'm afraid you can't test them here. A pity. This lot just arrived yesterday from England. No time to take them over to New Jersey. I must be off to Chicago this afternoon and you must be off to Texas. So you must take my word that this so-called Mexican grenade—Mr. Maxim improved on a basic Mexican Army design—has proved itself to be completely reliable."

All Garrity had to say to that was, "I'll know soon enough."

Chapter Two

The ticket agent at the Amarillo depot told Garrity it would be an hour and 15 minutes before the spur-line train from Lawton arrived. Then there would be another wait while the refrigerated meat cars were uncoupled and empty cars put in their place.

"Only one passenger car on the Lawton line," the ticket agent said. "Don't hardly need it. Not that much passenger business between here and there. Wasn't for the packing plant there'd be no rail line at all."

Two hours later, on the train heading for Lawton, Garrity looked out at the treeless, sunbaked grasslands of West Texas. It was summer and baking hot, but in winter the high plains got plenty of snow. Out there you fried or you froze. The great plateau ran all the way to the New Mexico line and beyond. The land was flat except for a few eroded river valleys.

Garrity hadn't seen the high plains for many years and that had been far to the south.

The packing plant train was no cannonball. Thirty miles an hour seemed to be good enough for the engineer or maybe he was under orders to stay at that speed. Refrigerated cars cost a lot of money. Kinnock was a wealthy man, but nothing compared to the great packing-plant operators up north. Train-wrecked refrigerators, as the cold cars were called, would make a big hole in his pocketbook. And he was having enough trouble as it was.

Reddish dust blew in the open windows of the train. If he wanted a breeze he had to put up with the dust. Only three other passengers were in the car: a salesman with a sample case, an old man with no luggage of any kind, a preacher with a leather grip and a Bible. No one spoke, for which Garrity was grateful. It was 75 miles from Amarillo to Lawton and he read a newspaper from first page to last before they were halfway there.

The light Maxim machine gun lay in its case on the floor. It was a weapon he trusted above all others. Without a doubt it was the best machine gun in the world. Many a time it had saved his life, many a man he had killed with it. When he first got it, it had been a standard Maxim light machine gun in the .303 caliber. The Maxim Company sold it as the Police Model and it was intended for use against rioters. It wasn't fitted with a water jacket, but the barrel was thick enough so 300 rounds could be fired in spaced bursts without any danger of overheating. Maxim Company gunsmiths had modified it according to his specifications. The heavy tripod had been replaced by a lightweight bipod fitted to the far end of the barrel. A steel-and-rubber grip had been attached to the underside of the gun, forward of the ammunition feed box. The gun had a pistol grip and a trigger. A single shot put the weapon on full automatic fire. The ammunition box could hold two canvas belts of 300 rounds. A shooter could lie behind it with the bipod extended. Or he could fire it from the hip, as Garrity sometimes did. Altogether, it was one hell of a gun.

The rest of his crated weapons were in the freight car. The name of a nonexistent meat processing equipment company was stenciled on the crates. Garrity was a salesman for this company if anybody asked. He didn't think he could get away with this for very long, but he had to have some excuse for being in a godforsaken town like Lawton, a place that saw few strangers. For what it was worth, it explained him, it explained all the crates.

He looked out the window until he got tired of the view. Not a tree, not a house or windmill broke the monotony of the plains, not that he minded. It was peaceful, so peaceful that he dozed off with his boots planted on top of the light-gun case.

He woke up before the train pulled into Lawton. Kinnock knew he was coming, but didn't know when. Garrity didn't want anybody meeting him at the depot, something a man like Kinnock would be sure to do. He wanted to take a look at the town before he went to the packing plant. No special reason for that, he just wanted to take a look. The three passengers got off at the depot and so did Garrity. Kinnock's meat factory was about 500 yards from the far end of town. The train went on to the company siding.

Garrity told the freight agent he'd be back to pick up his crates. He gave the man five dollars and was told, "I'll take good care of them, mister. First visit to Lawton?"

Garrity said yes.

"Town's got a great future," the agent said. "Some day we'll be as big as Amarillo, maybe bigger. You're going to like it here."

Garrity doubted that. A more miserable place he hadn't seen in a dog's age. A very old dog. There was just one street and that was mostly one sided and not very long. Strung out along the dusty street were a marshal's office, a few stores, a barbershop, a lumberyard that did funerals, a saloon, and a ramshackle hotel the Pinkerton agent had talked about. The hotel was the Lawton County headquarters of the United Workers of America. Next door to the hotel, across an alley, was the Good Times Saloon. Garrity was still spitting dust from the train ride. A big cold mug of beer was what he needed before he walked on down to the packing plant.

Four men were lounging on the splintered boardwalk in front of the saloon. Two were sitting on their heels, two were propping up the wall. They had the look of cowhands, but they all wore guns, something that wasn't so common anymore. Indian trouble was long in the past and the Pinkerton agent hadn't said anything about a range war in Lawton County. The men stared at Garrity as he pushed his way through the batwing doors and one of them muttered something that made the others laugh. Garrity ignored them. Every shitass town in the West had its share of bums.

No matter what the saloon called itself, the four men sitting at a table didn't look like they were having a good time. There were cards on the table, but they were playing for coins. This was no high-stakes game and they knew it and didn't like it. They were drinking beer instead of whiskey. Garrity thought

23

they looked like a sorry bunch, but like the men outside, they all wore guns.

The bartender took his time about coming up from the end of the bar to see what Garrity wanted. He asked for a bottle of Pearl beer and got it. After a few swipes at the bar with a dirty rag, the bartender went back to where he'd been talking to a mean-faced man of about 35 who had the look of a cowhand who had worked his way up to ramrod. He wore a Texas straw, Levi's with the ends rolled up, a blue denim shirt with the drawstring of a Bull Durham sack hanging out of the pocket. His gun rig was the fanciest thing about him—a soft leather, cartridge-studded, silver-stitched gunbelt and a holster with an open bottom. His pistol was a long-barreled Colt .45, single-action with an ivory handle. No cheap pearl for this waddy. He wanted the best. The barrel of the Colt stuck out through the open-end holster so people could see the front sight had been filed off, which meant he was so good with a gun he didn't need a sight or he wanted people to think he was.

Garrity was finishing his beer when the bartender came back. "Want another?"

"Maybe later," Garrity said. He picked up the gun case and turned to go, but the door was blocked by the four loungers he'd seen outside. Three were grinning, one was not, and they didn't step aside when he got close.

"Make way, gents," Garrity said. "Coming through."

The one who wasn't grinning said, "What's your hurry, mister? Me and the boys figured mebbe you might want to buy us a drink. Us fellers. You look like you got enough money to do that. You look like a drummer does all right for hisself."

The man who was bracing Garrity was young and small and wiry. He had small hands. His gun looked too big for such small hands.

"Make way," Garrity said. "You don't want any trouble with me."

The wiry little man smiled for the first time. Could be he didn't smile too much because he had no front teeth. "Course, we don't. We can be best friends after you buy us all that drink. I'd say you better do it."

Garrity's shoulder-holstered Sheriff's Model Colt .45 was pointing at his face before he could go on with his bullshit. It had a short barrel and the holster was greased. A real gunfighter might have got the drop on him, but this runt was nothing.

A voice behind Garrity said, "There's a gun on you, mister. Could break your spine at twice the distance. Drop the sneak gun and kick it away from you."

Garrity knew it was the man with the straw sombrero. He held the .45 steady on the little man's face. "I got the trigger squeezed and my thumb holding back the hammer. Shoot me in the back my thumb slips and your pal here gets a bullet in the face. How do you want it to go?"

Sweat ran down the little man's face. "For Christ's sake, Billy, let it go. We was just fooling."

Billy ignored him. "My gun is back in my holster," he told Garrity. "You put yours away and walk out of here."

Garrity's gunhand didn't move. "These men move out in front of me, drop their guns, then I'll leave."

Garrity knew the man called Billy might still shoot him in the back. Maybe he didn't like the runt all that much. One thing was for sure: Billy was the boss of this mangy bunch.

25

Billy took his time about answering. Then he said, "Do what he says, boys. Move out in front and turn loose the guns."

Four guns hit the floor and Garrity got behind the four men. Then he backed out of the saloon with the .45 still in his hand. He didn't ease down the hammer and put the gun away until he was well away from the saloon. But nobody came after him, nobody came out to see where he was going. No shots had been fired; so to the town he was just another salesman with a large sample case on his way to the packing plant. The few people on the forlorn street gawked at him, but then they gawked at anyone they hadn't seen before.

He passed the marshal's office. The marshal's name was Barrows and he had two deputies, Spoon and Wakely. They could be watching him from behind the barred windows of the jail. All strangers in troubled towns were suspect, but nobody with a badge stopped him to ask questions.

The packing plant was bigger than he expected, about half the size of a city block. It was built entirely of wood and had a galvanized iron roof. Cattle pens were at one end of it, a covered railroad siding at the other. The cattle were driven in at one end and came out the other as meat. A tall brick smokestack stuck up in the center of the building. That would be for the steam engines that powered the conveyor belts and other machinery. Two guards, both white, stood near an office door underneath a huge black-and-white sign emblazoned with Kinnock Meat Packing Company.

Garrity was glad to see the guards, though they didn't look like much. But at least Kinnock was taking some precautions. Two guards were better than no guards. One of them, the brighter looking of the two, asked him what his business was. Garrity said his business was with Kinnock and he was expected. He gave his name.

Kinnock himself came out after the bright guard checked. He was very tall and thin, with long sandy hair, a bushy untrimmed mustache and high cheekbones. Garrity knew he was 30, but he looked far older than that. Deacons usually didn't wear mustaches of any kind. Even so, there was a deaconish air about him. It was a hot day, but he was wearing the coat of his black basket-weave suit. His white shirt was buttoned up all the way. No tie.

"Mr. Garrity," he said gravely, shaking hands, "you should have sent me a telegram. I would have met you at the train." There was mild reproach in his voice. His accent was what Garrity took to be landed-gentry Scots, meaning that he didn't chew and mangle his words the way some Scotsmen did.

"I didn't want to bother you," Garrity said. "I know you're a busy man."

"Not too busy for common courtesy," Kinnock said. "But come in, sir, come in. I'm most pleased to see you. How is the colonel keeping himself?"

"The colonel's fine and sends his regards."

Kinnock led the way to his no-frills office. It was small with a desk, three hard chairs, four file cabinets and a coatrack. Tacked to the wall behind the plain wooden desk were a blueprint of the plant and a map of Lawton County. A heavily marked calendar bearing the name of some supply company was on the opposite wall.

Kinnock sat on his hard chair. "Would you like a wee drink after your long journey?"

"No thanks. I just had a beer at the saloon."

27

Kinnock frowned. "You're a grown man so I'll not lecture you, but that's a good place to stay out of. Few but rowdies drink there."

"Looks like it," Garrity said. "I had a run-in with a man they called Billy." Garrity described the man with the Texas straw and the long-barreled Colt. "You know him?"

"Aye," Kinnock said. "I know him all too well. That would be Billy Whittaker you're talking about. A real blackguard, that fellow. Worse than a blackguard. Whittaker is an ex-jailbird and some say a killer, though he's never been charged with any killing. But you came out of it all right."

"I persuaded Whittaker and his friends to let me be."

"You persuaded him?" Kinnock found that hard to believe.

"That's right. Some of Whittaker's friends, not Whittaker himself, tried to force me to buy them a drink. I had to show my gun to change their minds. Does that bother you, Mr. Kinnock?"

"No mister please. Plain Kinnock will do. Violence always bothers me, Garrity. I come from a race with a long history of bloodshed, but I take no pride in it. Oh well, you came out of it all right and that's all that matters. A word of advice though: steer clear of the Good Times and Billy Whittaker. And now we better have our talk. Suppose you lead off by telling me what you know of my situation."

Garrity had a copy of the Pinkerton agent's report in his pocket, but he didn't refer to it and he left out many things of no great importance. It was a long, painstaking report with everything in it but the kitchen sink. So he boiled it down and skimmed the hard facts off the top.

"That's it," Garrity said after talking for about five minutes with no interruptions from Kinnock. "That's what I know, what I've been told. You may not agree with all of it."

Kinnock was frowning. "We'll get to that in a minute. First I'd like to know where you got all this information?"

"Col. Pritchett hired the Pinkerton Detective Agency. They sent a man here posing as a land speculator. They picked that because it allowed him to talk to a lot of people. He was here a week."

"Aye, I heard about him all right." Kinnock was more annoyed than angry. "I ask you this: what business has Col. Pritchett sending detectives down here to spy on me? Why didn't he tell me? Damn his impertinence!"

"The colonel had—has—your best interests at heart. If he told you he was sending a Pink, you might have tried to put a stop to it."

"So I would," Kinnock said. "For the love of God, man, I'm thirty years old and have served in the Scots Guards. I didn't like the army, but it was expected that I serve like my father before me. Why does the colonel think I can't take care of myself?"

"That wasn't the idea," Garrity said. "Every man can use a helping hand. I'm always glad to get it. Why aren't you?"

Kinnock didn't answer that. "I really don't know the colonel, so why would he go to so much trouble on my behalf? It's not as if I served in his regiment. Maxim is behind this, isn't he?"

Garrity nodded. "So he is. What's wrong with that?"

"I don't like it. Is Maxim worried about his investment? It's a sizable investment, I admit, but it doesn't give him the right to pry into my affairs."

"Suppose we leave the indignation for later; then you can decide what you want to do. I'd be glad to have somebody as powerful as Maxim on my side, but it's your business if you're not. Now what about the Pinkerton report? Is it accurate?"

"Accurate for the most part, though I'm not sure the situation here is as serious as the agent seems to think it is. These private detectives sometimes exaggerate to make themself look good."

Garrity was beginning to think working with Kinnock would be a pain in the ass. He was a sanctimonious son of a bitch for somebody so young. And what the hell did he know about private detectives?

"It sounds pretty serious to me," Garrity said. "Another thing, the Pinkertons don't exaggerate. Old Pinkerton would skin their hides. Now you've had cattle stolen from your ranch. You've had your pens cleaned out here at the plant, not once but twice. Some of your workers and cowhands, black and white, have been beaten or threatened by the Klan. You yourself have been threatened with death if you don't pack up and get out. You don't think that's serious?"

"No one has been killed," Kinnock said, setting his long Scots jaw in a stubborn line.

"Not yet. The killing will come. So far Mayfield has just been testing your nerve. The report says he used to be a congressman and a lawyer who never practiced, which means he knows the law and would rather force you out by intimidation instead of killing and burning."

"Intimidation!" Kinnock scoffed at the idea. "He's wasting his time if that's what he's thinking. I'll not be forced out by a villain like that."

"The killing and burning will come," Garrity said. "Maybe sooner than you think. The Pinkerton man got hints that Mayfield is getting impatient."

This time Kinnock actually smiled a brief sour smile. "How did he manage that? Did Mayfield do the hinting?"

"He never got to talk to Mayfield. He got word, sort of, from a drunken Klansman late at night at the Good Times. Nobody there but the two of them and the bartender and he was busy rolling in beer kegs for the next day. The drunk said there was a meeting at Mayfield's barn, and Mayfield said it was time to teach this foreign Scotchman a lesson."

Kinnock continued to sit straight in his hard chair. He wasn't one for leaning forward or tilting back. "Was this agent buying him drinks?"

"Sure," Garrity said. "That's how it's done. They drink, they talk. Sometimes they do."

"Then he probably told the agent what he wanted to hear. Something dramatic that he could put into his report."

"That could be," Garrity admitted. "The agent mentioned that as a possibility, but added that the Klansman was as dumb as dirt and probably wouldn't make up a story like that. What does it matter if he did or not? You have the evidence of your own eyes. You know what's happened. So far Mayfield's been just baring teeth. It follows that next time, maybe not so far off, he'll take a big bite out of you or out of your men. For instance, what's to stop him from burning this place?" Garrity meant the packing plant.

"I've posted guards," Kinnock said irritably. "Two guards by day, four at night."

31

"Not enough, especially the night guards. Four men can't guard a place this big. The cattle pens alone should have four guards. How many cattle did you lose in the two raids?"

"About seven hundred. What do you want me to do, Garrity? Hire gunmen?"

"It's not a bad idea," Garrity said. "But I guess you wouldn't consider it?"

"Not for a moment." Kinnock spoke as if the words were engraved on a marble slab.

Maybe he'll be under another kind of marble slab if he doesn't start using his head, Garrity thought. Like it or not, it was his job to keep the bullheaded Scotsman alive in spite of himself.

"Let me ask you a question," Garrity said. "For the sake of argument, what would you do if, say, Mayfield's Klansmen burned this plant?"

"Why would he burn valuable property he plans to take over?"

"He might think it was worth it if it got rid of you. He might do it if everything else failed. I don't know Mayfield, but my information is that he's a very practical man. He'd rather take over a thriving business than a pile of ashes and wrecked machinery. But Mayfield is greedy as well as practical. My guess is his greed will win out. That, I figure, will be any day now."

Suddenly Kinnock's face was tight with impatience. "At the risk of being rude, let me say that I didn't ask Col. Pritchett for help, but now that you're here, what do you propose to do?"

"Look around, see for myself what you're up against. See if Mayfield can't be persuaded to call off his mangy dogs."

"The way you persuaded Whittaker and his thugs?"

"I'm glad you see them as thugs and not high-spirited yokels. Guns are all these vicious bastards understand. If I have to persuade Mayfield with a gun, that's what I'll do."

Garrity listened to the thud of machinery while Kinnock decided what he was going to say. Finally Kinnock said, "What if I refuse to cooperate?"

"That would make things harder, but it wouldn't stop me. I don't work for you. I work for Col. Pritchett. You can't stop me from nosing around, you can't run me out of town. Listen to me, Kinnock, I'm not here to make things worse. I'll let you know what I'm doing all the time." Garrity was lying about the last part. "You don't like what I'm doing you can show me the door."

Kinnock did some more heavy thinking. "All right," he decided. "Let's leave it at that . . . for now."

With that out of the way, Garrity said, "What about these United Workers of America organizers? The Pinkerton report says they've been giving you trouble. Trying to organize your plant workers the hard way. How rough have they been?"

It looked like Kinnock had to think out everything he said. Maybe that was just his Scottish caution, Garrity thought. Maybe he talked more freely when a man got to know him better.

"Durkin, their leader, talks very tough," Kinnock said. "The man is a labor thug who's seen the inside of any number of jails. I know because he boasts about it. I tried to explain that I pay my plant workers better wages than they'd get anywhere else. I showed him the bunkhouses I provide for single men with no homes of their own. I showed him the good quality of their food. I told him my workers, black and white, are treated and paid the same. Nothing impressed him. He said that was a lot of paternalistic bullshit—the fellow has read a book or two—and my plant would be organized come hell or high water. His very words. Since then he and his thuggish organizers have been going after my men wherever they find them. No violence as yet, but in my opinion they're as bad as the Klan."

Garrity didn't think that was quite true. The UWOA organizers were a tough bunch, but they weren't as bad as the Klan. True, they had dynamited a few iron-fisted mine operators up in the Northwest, but not all the bombings were their work. Some were police frame-ups. Guilty or innocent, three UWOA leaders had been hanged on flimsy evidence.

"How do they get on with the Klan?" Garrity asked, knowing the answer, but wanting to hear how Kinnock saw it. "It's a wonder the Klan doesn't try to run them out of town."

A second sour smile from Kinnock. "Not these fellows. They're armed to the teeth and afraid of nothing. The Klan walks softly around them and so does the marshal. But it has to come to a showdown, I'm afraid. Meanwhile, I have to contend with both factions. Oh well, I'm sure it will sort itself out. Why don't we talk later at the ranch? You'll be staying at the ranch, naturally. Is that all the luggage you have?" Kinnock meant the gun case.

"'Fraid not," Garrity said. "I have at least two wagonloads of stuff waiting to be picked up at the depot."

"Indeed." Kinnock was puzzled but too polite to ask questions. "You certainly don't travel light."

"Can you manage two wagons?"

"Certainly. I'll tell my head teamster. Now if you'll wait thirty minutes or so we'll be on our way. Some things I must attend to."

"I'll walk down to the depot ahead of you," Garrity said.

Chapter Three

The door of the marshal's office was open and Garrity was walking past it when a rasping voice called out, "Hold it right there, mister. We got two sawed-offs and a pistol on you. Hands up high."

Garrity put his hands up and two deputies with sawed-offs at hip level came out followed by the marshal. The marshal had a cocked pistol in his hand. Both deputies were young, the marshal well into middle age, a jowly man with a thick waist and a grizzled mustache clipped short. The deputies looked like cowhands who had found a soft job in hard times.

"What goes on? What's the trouble?" Garrity said. By now the three men were behind him. The marshal stepped forward and took his gun.

"You're under arrest for attempted murder," the marshal said. "Turn nice and easy and walk into the jail. Try anything and you're a dead man."

Garrity turned slowly and saw Billy Whittaker standing in the door of the jail. Whittaker's left arm was in a bloodstained sling. He stepped back when Garrity came through. One of the three cells facing the marshal's desk was open and the marshal prodded him into it, then slammed the gate and turned the key. The marshal and the deputies remained standing in the center of the room. Whittaker stood with his back against the wall, near the door.

"What the hell is this all about?" Garrity said, knowing damn well what it was all about. "I didn't attempt to murder anybody."

Marshal Barrows looked at him with dead eyes. "You attempted to murder Billy Whittaker there. Lucky for him and lucky for you all he got was a bullet wound in the arm. Otherwise you'd be facing a hanging charge. As it is, mister, you'll be going to state prison for a long, long time."

Garrity stayed back from the bars. One of the deputies had edged close enough to try to smash him in the face with the shotgun butt.

The marshal sat behind his desk and opened a large, worn book with leather corners. He dipped a pen in an inkwell and looked at Garrity. "Full name and address and what you do for a living. No lies, no bullshit."

Garrity gave his right name and the address of the Denver hotel where he often stayed between jobs. He said he worked for the Herman Obermeyer Company of Cincinnati. "Meat processing machines, meat saws, knives." The marshal wrote it all down, scowling as if he didn't believe a word of it, as Garrity said, "Why would a salesman want to shoot anybody?"

Marshal Barrows said, "I don't know the why of it, but you did shoot Whittaker."

"If he got shot then he shot himself or made it look like he'd been shot."

Whittaker lurched away from the wall with his hand close to his gun. "You know you shot me, you lying son of a bitch. You wouldn't have shot me if I'd been ready for you. Let me have him, Marshal. Five minutes. I'll beat the truth out of him."

The marshal clicked his fingers and the two deputies took Whittaker's gun and pushed him back against the wall. "Simmer down, you hear me," the marshal said. "The law will take care of this so-called salesman."

Garrity got the feeling that the aging marshal would rather be tilted back in his swivel chair, reading the paper with his boots on the desk, a good cigar in his mouth. Probably that's what he'd be doing if this Klan trouble hadn't started up.

"If I fired at Whittaker," Garrity said, "how come you didn't hear the shot? My gun is a .45 and you're just a few doors away. You couldn't have missed that much noise."

"I was riding back to town at the time," the marshal said. "I checked the time. That's where I was, me and my deputies." The marshal's lie made him mad and he shouted, "Don't you be asking me questions, slicker. I'll ask the questions round here. You did it, sure as shit. Billy Whittaker was bleeding like a stuck pig when he come in here and showed me the arm wound. I washed it and bandaged it. We got no doctor in this town. You trying to tell me I didn't see what I saw?"

"Maybe you saw some kind of a wound. Wouldn't be hard to fake a bullet crease with a rough piece of metal. I would say Whittaker's wound isn't too serious. Anyway, my gun wasn't the cause of it. Smell the barrel of my gun. It hasn't been fired."

Garrity's gun was on the marshal's desk, but he didn't touch it. "You had plenty of time to clean it and load a new shell on the way to the meat factory."

"I'm telling you I didn't shoot anybody." Garrity knew he was wasting his time. "Where's the profit in shooting a stranger, a man I never saw before? Why didn't his pals throw down on me, eight of them, one of me?"

"Because you look like a gunslinger. They're just cowhands not gun sharpies. So is Whittaker."

Garrity wondered how bad it was going to get. They could beat the shit out of him and nothing would happen. They could kill him just as easily. The story would be that he grabbed a gun and got killed in the struggle to take it away from him.

He decided to see what effect Kinnock's name would have. "Lord Kinnock isn't going to like this. He knows my company and knows they don't employ gunmen. Why would they? For what reason? I wrote to Lord Kinnock and I'm here by his invitation."

Marshal Barrows scratched the bristles on his two chins. "To show your wares, is that it?"

"That's right."

"Anyway, that's what you say. Maybe you think you can lie to me because you think I'm just a hick-town marshal. Wrong. I was ten years a patrolman in Dallas before I got this job. In that time I seen maybe a thousand drummers, every kind of drummer there is, and you don't look like any of them. You don't look like one, you don't talk like one. By the way, slicker, where's that sample case you was carrying when you left the saloon?"

"At the meat plant," Garrity said. "I thought I'd walk around, look at the town while Lord Kinnock finished up some business. Then we were going out to his ranch."

"Pretty close, you and his lordship." The marshal's fat face twisted itself into a sneer. "You listen good because I'm going to tell you something maybe you didn't know. Throwing Kinnock's name at me don't mean shit. That foreigner may be a high muckymuck back in Scotland. Here he's just somebody that sells meat."

"He's bigger than that, Marshal."

"Not to me he ain't. The law is the law, the same for a lord as a saloon swamper. You're in a bad fix and nobody's going to get you out of it. What say you cut out the bullshit and tell the real reason you're in Lawton County. You can make it easy or hard, but you're going to tell the truth. Your choice."

"I'm just a salesman," Garrity said. "You can beat me bloody, but I'll still be a salesman when you get through."

The marshal shrugged. "We'll see."

The two deputies moved toward the cell. Both were grinning. The one the marshal called Spoon picked the key up off the desk. Wakely, the other one, was pulling on leather gloves. Spoon was fitting the key into the lock when somebody banged on the door. The banging got louder when there was no response. Then a reedy voice called out, "Open the door, Marshal, it's Wesley Torrance. You hear me, Marshal? Lawyer Torrance. Let me in. I want to see my client. I know he's in there."

"I'm in here!" Garrity shouted as loud as he could.

"Let the bastard in," the marshal said.

Spoon unlocked the door and the lawyer came in followed by Kinnock, who was carrying the gun case.

Garrity was surprised that a sinkhole like Lawton had enough work for a lawyer, and this one didn't look like he was new in town. He was about 60, not tall, with long white hair brushed back straight from his forehead. Unlike many village lawyers who lived from hand to mouth, he didn't look like a drinker or a toady. There was nothing seedy about him. His gray sack suit wasn't new but it was well looked after. Maybe he had a little money, maybe a lot.

"Ah, there's my client," Wesley Torrance said. "Treating you all right, Mr. Garrity?" His faded but shrewd blue eyes didn't miss Wakely's leather gloves.

"So far, Mr. Torrance," Garrity said, thinking maybe he had a chance of getting out of this.

"Since when is this man your client?" For the first time, the marshal looked unsure of himself. But he had gone along with the false charge and was trying to brazen it out.

Torrance smiled. "Since Kinnock hired me a few minutes ago. What's my client charged with?"

"Attempted murder. He shot Billy Whittaker there. Your client's got to be held till he's taken over to the county seat to stand trial."

Torrance took a sideways look at Whittaker. "Circuit judge won't sit for a month from now, as you well know. So Billy's signed a complaint, has he? Since when do you take the word of a twice-convicted felon. A two-time jailbird. Billy can't vote, can't sit on a jury."

From behind the two deputies Whittaker shouted, "Mr. Mayfield is working to get me a full pardon."

The marshal told him to be quiet. Torrance said, "The day that man gets a pardon is the day I quit Texas for good. Marshal, you can't take the word of a man like that, a bully and a liar. Billy Whittaker

41

is the bottom of the barrel, the absolute dregs."

Whittaker tried to get past the deputies, but they pushed him back. The lawyer remained calm. "See, Marshal," he said. "Mayfield's pet thug is ready to beat up a sixty-year-old man with high blood pressure and arthritis. Next he'll be stomping one-legged grandmothers. I'd like to hear the charge explained in more detail, but first I'd like to remind you Whittaker was sent to prison, first for rape, later for trying to castrate a man whose woman he coveted. Mayfield whispered in the judge's ear and he got two years instead of twenty."

"All that has nothing to do with this," the marshal blustered. "Whittaker has legal rights same as anybody else."

"Tell me about the charges, Marshal."

Marshal Barrows told how Whittaker had come to the jail bleeding like a stuck pig from a bullet wound in the upper left arm. "Me and the boys had just walked in when Whittaker arrived. If I'd been here I would have heard the shot and gone to see what the trouble was. I fixed up Whittaker's arm the best I could and he signed the complaint. We found Garrity and arrested him."

Torrance smiled. "It's all so neat."

"That's how it happened. Garrity has to stand trial."

"We'll see. Now about this gunshot wound poor Whittaker is supposed to have suffered? I guess you know a gunshot wound when you see one, having been a lawman for close on twenty-five years."

"Closer to thirty," the marshal said.

Torrance nodded. "Thirty years it is. You must have seen your share of gunshot wounds in your three decades as a lawman. And you have no doubt that Whittaker's wound was inflicted by a bullet?"

The argument was between the lawyer and the marshal, Garrity thought. It was obvious that the two old men had locked horns in the past and were still at it.

"No doubt at all," the marshal said. "Whittaker was wounded by a bullet." The marshal looked as if he wanted to be at the other end of Texas.

Torrance wasn't bothered by the marshal's statement. "We'll see what a doctor has to say about that. A real doctor, not a drunken or an incompetent doctor, but a highly respected doctor. Dr. Phail up in Amarillo is just the man for the job. I'll get on the telegraph right away. We're old friends and he'll be on the next train soon as he hears from me."

"Do what you like." The marshal was red faced but defiant.

Torrance said, "It won't look so good for you if Doc Phail decides the wound was made by a sharp stick or something rough edged like a stove-lid lifter. It could get into the county newspaper. I'll see that it does. Think of the jokes, Marshal. What won't be a joke will be my telegram to Gov. Ross. You beat my client and you'll answer to him. The governor and I went to law school together."

For a bad moment Garrity thought the marshal was going to let Torrance walk out of there and to hell with the doctor, the newspaper, the governor. Kinnock was opening the door when the marshal said, "Wait a minute. Let's talk this over."

Torrance turned to face him. "Very well. Let us reason together."

Marshal Barrows shifted in his chair. His ass seemed to be as uncomfortable as the expression on his face. "It ain't up to me," he said. "I got no doubts your client shot Whittaker, but the wound ain't what you'd call serious and maybe there was a misunderstanding. It's plain this man can't take a joke. Billy Whittaker and the boys are all right, but their tomfoolery can get out of hand."

"Boys will be boys," the lawyer said amiably.

The marshal looked at Whittaker. "How about it, Billy? There's no denying you been shot. But you want to drag through a trial with our slick lawyer friend here and maybe the doc saying you wasn't wounded by no bullet?"

Whittaker cleared his throat and looked ready to spit a gob on the floor. A sharp look from the marshal changed his mind and he swallowed it. "The Amarillo doc'd be a liar if he said that. Fuck it! They's no way a poor man can win against weasel lawyers and fancy-talking doctors. Who'd believe me? Let it drop, Marshal."

"A wise decision," Torrance said.

"You watch your step, mister," the marshal said when he let Garrity out.

The jail door slammed behind them. Everybody in town was gawking at them, openly or through dusty windows. "Well that wasn't too hard," the lawyer said, pleased with himself. "But you'd better take care, Mr. Garrity. The marshal's been bested, so he probably won't try again. Whittaker, on the other hand, is as mean as a cottonmouth, and there is no meaner snake. God knows what crimes—some of them bushwhack murders—he hasn't been caught at. I'm pretty sure he murdered the only Chinaman in Lawton County. Poor Oriental ran a five-stool chop-suey parlor. Just a shack he built himself." The lawyer pointed to the other side of the street. "That pile of charred boards is all that's left of it. Whittaker and his Klansmen figured the poor bastard had money. They tortured him and then cut his throat."

44

"Thanks for getting me out," Garrity said, not too interested in dead Chinamen. "They'd have stomped me flat if you hadn't showed up."

"I saw Wakely's bullyboy gloves. No need to thank me. I'm getting paid. Thank Kinnock."

"You weren't at the depot so I started looking," Kinnock said. "The barber told me you'd been arrested. Mr. Torrance was kind enough to take your case."

"Kind nothing," Torrance said. "I need the money."

Kinnock's buckboard was hitched in front of the jail. "I had my teamsters take your boxes out to the ranch. I didn't know how long you'd be locked up."

"Fine," Garrity said.

"Kinnock," the lawyer said. "Would you mind if I have a word with Garrity in private? Counsel to client, so to speak."

"What?" Kinnock looked slightly annoyed, but he said, "It will give me a chance to look in at the lumberyard."

Garrity picked up the gun case and followed the lawyer up the stairs to his three-room office and living quarters, which were above a hardware store. The office had pine paneling stained dark brown. His college and law school diplomas hung in frames above rows of law books on open shelves. The desk and the leather couch were old and well used. There was a faint smelling of cooking.

Garrity said no thanks to a drink and sat on the uncomfortable couch because the two visitor's chairs were piled high with books. Torrance hung his coat on the back of his desk chair and sat in it.

"You know, you're lucky to be alive," he said.

Jack Slade

"Is Whittaker that good with a gun?" Garrity wondered what the lawyer wanted to talk about. "He wears his gun like he thinks he is."

"That's mostly for show, but I guess he's good enough. He was in several range wars after he was released from prison the second time. That was down around Lubbock. I guess he did his gun work all too well. The last rancher that hired him ran him off, told him he'd be killed if he didn't go. He came back here and eventually landed a job with Pig Meat Mayfield. Mayfield is. . . ."

"I know who he is," Garrity said.

Torrance showed no surprise. "Then you're certainly not a salesman."

"I'm here to help Kinnock. He says he doesn't need help."

"That sounds like Kinnock," the lawyer said. "It's Kinnock I want to talk about. I won't ask you what you are, though I have a fair idea. What I'd like to know is if you've known Kinnock long. Do you have any influence over him?"

"None at all. I just met him today."

"That's too bad. Somebody's got to talk some sense into him. He'll be killed for sure if he doesn't stop believing in the essential goodness of man. Sweet reason hardly ever works and it doesn't work at all in West Texas. The trouble with Kinnock is he thinks good works will make Lawton County a better place. He thinks the poor whites will stop hating blacks if he gives them jobs and pays them well so they won't be eating reheated beans and sow belly three times a day. Rid them of their resentment and anger is his idea. What he doesn't seem to realize is they hate the blacks worse than ever—and they hate him—because he makes them work alongside blacks and gives them the same

46

pay, which is heresy by West Texas, any Texas, standards."

"I know that," Garrity said.

"The real sticky part," the lawyer said, "is the whites would like to quit their jobs, but the pay is too good. These are hard times and if they quit they'll have to go back to the beans and belly. So the way they see it is this: Kinnock is forcing them to work with niggers, and that's more than enough to make them hate him. I wouldn't be surprised if some of them had a hand in the two raids on his cow pens."

"I thought of that, Mr. Torrance."

"You'd think the poor whites would be grateful now that they have decent food in their bellies, a few dollars in their pockets. Like hell they are. I'm not sure some of them don't belong to Mayfield's Klan. I know that sounds crazy, but it's my experience that most people are crazy in one way or another. You know, people have been fouling their own nests since the Garden of Eden. For instance, what is a man like Lord Kinnock doing in a godforsaken place like West Texas? Why isn't he hunting deer in the Highlands? If he wants to do good, why doesn't he do it to the half-starved crofters of Scotland? Let's leave Kinnock for a moment. What in hell are these United Workers of America organizers doing here? Other than the packing plant there is absolutely no industry here. The population is sparse and mostly illiterate. By the way, did Kinnock tell you that these labor organizers have been making trouble for him?"

"He did. You think it will come to open violence."

"I wouldn't be surprised if it did. That fellow Durkin, their boss, is a fearsome-looking character. Lost an eye in the labor wars and instead of wearing an eye patch he had some quack sew up the empty socket. Did a lousy job of it. Doctor must have been drunk or else he used a mailbag needle. The Irish bastard is determined to organize Kinnock's plant whether the workers like it or not. Then he plans to go after the big ranchers that employ a lot of men. Men like Kinnock and Pig Meat Mayfield. So far he hasn't bothered Mayfield. Durkin may be a thug, but he's a smart thug. He says he'll go after Mayfield when he's ready. My Lord! And this used to be such a quiet hole in the wall."

Garrity thought of asking Torrance why he stayed on, but decided not to. Instead, he said, "Durkin will have to be as tough as he talks to take on the Klan."

"I think he's tough enough. My guess is he's waiting for the Klan to fire the first shot. That will give him the excuse he needs."

"How many men does he have?"

"Twelve, but they're all as tough as he is. They're well armed and afraid of nothing. They're outnumbered by the Klan, not that numbers mean a whole lot. A good many Klansmen are gutless malcontents who whine better than they fight. Not all of them though. There's a hard core of men like Billy Whittaker, so Durkin won't find it so easy to put them down. You know Durkin has called a public meeting for nine o'clock tonight?"

"I saw some kind of painted banner over the hotel door, but the wind had tangled it up."

"They'll have it untangled and nailed down by now," Torrance said. "Yes indeed. Durkin's holding an open air meeting so he can tell the yokels what his union can do for them and at the same time denounce Kinnock and the Klan and capitalists in general. Will be the most entertainment this miserable town has had since old man Morfit ran naked down the street in a fit of delirium tremens."

"Are you going to be there?"

"Wouldn't miss it for the world. What about Kinnock? Will he be in attendance?"

"He said nothing about it to me," Garrity said. "He said we'd drive out to his ranch when he got through for the day. Maybe I'll ask him. To get back to what you wanted to discuss, what do you think Kinnock should do?

"Be more careful," the lawyer said. "He needs a bodyguard, maybe more than one man. He drives all over in that buckboard of his. Anybody could take a shot at him and never be caught, not that Marshal Barrows would try too hard. Sometimes he works till late at the plant, then drives home alone. He's going to get killed if he doesn't take more care."

"I'll do my best to convince him. Is that it?" Garrity said.

Torrance looked a little uneasy. "Not entirely. I don't know how to put this, but it has to be said for Kinnock's own good. Fact is, there would be no trouble if not for the blacks. He made a mistake there. It's not that he has blacks working for him. It's how he's got them working for him. Nobody would care a hell of a lot if he hired blacks, but kept them separate and didn't pay them equal wages. He could still do that. The blacks might grumble, but they'd still be making more money than they'd make anywhere else. I guess you think I'm a real son of a bitch to put it like that? I'm not, you know. The way I see it, there'll be work for nobody if that plant is burned down, which is likely to happen one of these nights. Just as bad—no, worse—there will be wholesale killing if the present situation doesn't change. What do you think?"

Jack Slade

"I don't think you're a son of a bitch. Everything you say is true, but it's kind of wrong to take it out on the blacks. Poor bastards have been shit on for years. I've got nothing for or against blacks, but it seems kind of mean to try to lift them up, as Kinnock has done, and then knock them down again. Anyway, Kinnock would never go along with it."

Torrance sighed in exasperation. "I figured you were going to say that. Well, sir, I tried, hoping you could persuade him to look at the situation in a realistic way. I can't help him. Do what you can, Garrity. He's a decent man, but he's not of this world. I'd hate to see him dead on a dark road."

"Me too," Garrity said. "Kinnock is a crank, but I'll do my best for him."

"Don't you get killed either," the lawyer said.

Chapter Four

Kinnock was sitting in the buckboard when Garrity came down from the lawyer's office. Garrity expected the other man to ask about the meeting, but Kinnock said, "I say, would you mind if we didn't drive out to the ranch for a few hours? That fellow Durkin is holding a meeting this evening and I'd like to hear what he has to say. If you're tired and hungry we can skip it."

Garrity said he wasn't tired and they could probably get something to eat in town. "I saw some kind of restaurant."

"My initial decision was to ignore the blackguard, but I've changed my mind. It would be thin-skinned on my part not to attend. Let him rant and rave as much as he likes. Sticks and stones, and so on. What harm can he do to me?"

Maybe a lot of harm, Garrity thought, but he said,

"I always enjoy listening to rabble-rousers. They're better than actors."

Kinnock didn't like Garrity's light tone. "I don't find Durkin the least bit entertaining. Ah well, let us get something to eat. We'll have a decent supper when we get home tonight."

To get to the eating place Garrity had seen they had to pass Durkin's headquarters. The wind-tangled canvas sign had been secured by nails. Two men stood on the porch, one of them the most beat-up man Garrity had ever seen. Battered but not beaten down. The badly stitched eye socket identified him as Durkin, the wild man from the Northwest. His face was lumped and scarred and it had white patches as if burned in a fire. Part of his left ear was missing; maybe it had been bitten off in some savage fight. The real savage brawlers were known to bite off ears and noses if fists and feet failed. Compared to Durkin, the other man looked normal, just an average head-beating labor bully. Neither of them spoke.

"That was Durkin," Kinnock said a few moments later. "The one missing an eye."

"He sure is no beauty," Garrity said.

The restaurant had a false front that creaked in the wind. Inside, it was bigger than it looked, with five stools along a counter and five tables in back. Two men were eating at the counter. No one was at the tables. Garrity and Kinnock got a table and the man who doubled as cook and counterman came to take their orders. They ordered ham and eggs, safe enough food in a place like that, and a pot of coffee.

"Think Durkin will get much of a crowd?" Garrity said, looking at the two men at the counter. They hadn't been in the saloon with Whittaker; they weren't wearing guns.

"Not as big a crowd as at the last meeting," Kinnock said. "The Klan has been busy since then, trying to scare people off. But some people will turn out in spite of the Klan. Some of my own plant workers will be there. It's hard to say how many."

The two men at the counter paid up and left, one a few minutes after the other. From down the street there was the sound of hammering.

"They're putting up the speaker's platform," Kinnock said.

"Sounds like it," Garrity said.

After the counterman brought the food and went back to the kitchen, Garrity said, "I guess you'd like to know what Torrance talked about?"

Kinnock looked embarrassed. "Only if you want to tell me."

"He thinks you should take better care of yourself. Hire a bodyguard, maybe a couple of bodyguards. The man is right. He thinks your whole setup at the plant is a mistake. Putting blacks alongside whites, working for the same wages. He thinks you should put the blacks in a separate section and pay them somewhat lower wages. He thinks that would probably stop the Klan trouble. What do you think?"

Kinnock's long face didn't show much of anything. "What do you think? I'm a plain man and I like plain words."

"I said that would be a mean thing to do."

"But you didn't say it shouldn't be done?"

"That's right. It's not up to me. And it's just possible that some of your blacks took part in the cow stealing and the breaking of machinery. Men, black or white, will do anything for money."

"That's hard to believe," Kinnock said.

"Believe it," Garrity said. "You think blacks will turn into upstanding citizens if they get the right chance. That's true for the most part. Just the same, there are blacks just as rotten as the worst white man. Face it, Kinnock, not all lynched blacks are innocent. Now and then they do rape and murder white women."

Kinnock's red face got redder. "For God's sake, you're talking like a Klansman."

"No, sir, I'm just stating the facts. Not all white women are raped, but they holler rape if they're caught with a black man with his pants down."

Kinnock was appalled. "Now you're talking like a blackguard."

"Not so. Just putting it as blunt as I could. The point is that not all your blacks are downtrodden angels."

"But surely the Klan wouldn't have anything to do with negroes other than flog or hang them."

"The Klan would work with Jew-Catholic blacks if it suited their purpose. But let's pass on that for now. All I'm saying is you shouldn't be taken in by sunny smiles and big displays of loyalty. Trust nobody."

Kinnock pushed his food around on his plate. "That would be a sad way to live." He drank some of the bad coffee before he said anything else. Then he said, "Do you think Torrance's suggestion—if I agreed to it—would stop my trouble with the Klan?"

"Not a chance. Mayfield wants your plant and your ranch, so he'll keep coming at you. Worse than that, if you segregated your workers he'd take it as a sign of weakness."

Kinnock gave up on his hard fried eggs and gristly ham and pushed the plate away. "I'm glad you said that because I have no intention of doing it. Sink or swim, my plant will go on the way it's been going. I know the Klansmen hate my guts, but at least that's out in the open. It's the townspeople who bother me. It's as if they look at me out of the corners of their eyes and whisper behind my back. Why do you think they're so hostile?"

"You want me to say it plain, so I will. The merchants, the rest of them, like the money you've brought to this miserable town. That doesn't mean they like you. I'm not saying they hate you like the Klan does. It's just that you're different, a foreigner in a place with few foreigners. In West Texas that's enough. If you succeed you'll make big money while they'll always be small-timers. Have you ever thought of selling for a good price and moving, say, to Montana? No blacks there, no Klan. Look at it straight, Kinnock. Mayfield could drive you out in time."

"I'd sell out for half my investment before I'd let that happen."

"That would just be putting off Mayfield's takeover. He'd force the new owner out in no time."

"I wasn't talking about selling to a West Texas man. I meant some big rancher or combination of businessmen, not necessarily Texans. Big, tough, powerful men who wouldn't give a damn for Mayfield and his hooded thugs. But I have no intention of selling to anyone. This is my adopted country and state and I intend to be buried here."

Garrity had nothing to say about the burying part. It wasn't dark yet, but it was getting there. He looked at his watch. "Quarter to nine," he said. "You want to stroll on down and see what's happening?"

"Yes," Kinnock said. "I want to be in the front row when the swine starts tearing into me." He tried to make it sound casual, but Garrity knew he was all tensed up.

A small crowd had already gathered. More were

on their way, Garrity figured. Few meetings started on time. The platform had been bolted together and there was red, white and blue bunting suspended between tall poles. A long table with chairs behind it was set up at the front of the platform and the papers on it were weighted down with rocks against the night wind.

Durkin was on the platform giving orders in a rough voice. Garrity noticed that his right ear was cauliflowered and wondered if he had been a prizefighter before he joined the labor movement. Men like Durkin worked at many trades, all of them rough. He wasn't any taller than the other organizers, but his lean, hard body and aggressive manner seemed to make him taller. He looked up and his pale gray eye, the good one, narrowed when Garrity and Kinnock pushed their way to the front. Then he sat in the middle chair and looked at the papers on the table.

Four chairs were on the platform, which meant that only four men would be speaking. Garrity knew the eight other union men would be standing guard on the porch, at the upstairs windows, maybe on the roof. That meant rifles and shotguns, and the lawyer said they knew how to use them. Garrity was thinking about that when Torrance joined them in the front row. In contrast to Kinnock, the lawyer was as calm as a contented grandmother knitting socks for her grandchildren.

The crowd was getting bigger. It was past nine and getting close to dark. One of the organizers touched a match to the portable carbide lamps that hung from the poles supporting the bunting. The two lamps flared up bright, throwing harsh white light on the crowd and the platform. Three men who were to sit with Durkin came out of the hotel and took their places. They sat with impassive faces while Durkin continued to shuffle through his papers.

"Odd thing," the lawyer said. "Maybe not so odd. There's no sign of the marshal and his deputies. They're not at the jail, not in the crowd, nowhere close to the crowd—and their horses are gone. I know. I looked. Maybe you should go on home, Kinnock."

Kinnock stared at the lawyer. "Why should I? Perhaps the marshal and his men are watching the approaches to the town."

Torrance shrugged. "That could be, but in my opinion that's no way to police a potentially violent meeting. Another thing: there are no Klansmen in the crowd. I know most of them and they're not here. Fact is about half the crowd is made up of men who work for you."

"My workers are free to do what they please." Kinnock sounded pious and, to Garrity, pretty goddamn stupid. Or maybe he didn't want to understand what the lawyer was trying to tell him.

"My advice is for you to go home right now," Torrance said. "There could be trouble here tonight and you're up front right under the bright lights."

Garrity stooped to unlock the gun case, then moved it in front of him. He made it look as if he didn't want the case to be damaged by men pushing from the back. The crowd was getting impatient and a man shouted from the back, "Hey, Durkin, when is this show going to start?"

Other men joined in the yelling, but mostly it was good-natured.

Kinnock said, "If you think there's going to be trouble, why are you here, Mr. Torrance?"

The lawyer was a man who smiled a lot, but that time he didn't. "I came here to warn you," he said.

"You do what you like, sir, and now I'm going to watch this thing from a safe distance. First sign of trouble I'll be home behind a locked door with a shotgun on my desk. Good night to both of you."

"That fellow is like an old woman," Kinnock said. Just then Durkin stood up and held out his hands for silence. He looked even uglier under the harsh lights. Garrity knew he was armed, but his gun didn't show. Same thing with the other men at the table. Garrity could see four men with shotguns standing back in the shadows of the wide porch.

"Fellow workers!" Durkin started with a shout and kept on shouting. "I bid you welcome. I wish there were enough of you to fill a football field. I wish—"

Somebody in back called out, "We're a small county, Mr. Durkin."

"Button your lip, dunderdick!" Durkin shouted back. "You want to talk, then come up on the platform and do it. Any man that wants to talk can come up here and do it. Free speech! Good solid jobs, fair wages, shorter hours, no kowtowing to the fat-gut bosses, all men equal. That's what the United Workers of America is all about and we want to see it not in some rosy distant future, but right now. No more promises, no more bullshit, no more pie-in-the-sky. We want action now! Am I getting through to you, working men of Lawton County? Are you with me? Are you ready to get up off your knees and start acting like men? No offense meant by what I just said, but you know as well as I do that kissing the boss's asshole looks like the only thing you can do when you have no work or the job you have stinks, when you're hungry and your family is hungry. But it doesn't have to be like that. Right now it's like that because you're disorganized, with one man pitted against the other, fighting to get a dirty job or trying to hang on to the dirty job you have when there should be plenty of decent jobs for all. They say there's a depression going on. Let me explain what a depression is. It's when the bosses decide to put the squeeze on the working man. It's when the bosses decide to fuck around with the stock market, when they decide to force small companies out of business and hundreds of thousands of working men out of a job. Now I don't give a shit about small companies because to me all employers are the enemy! Maybe we need them right now, but I'd like to see there come a time when everything is run by the working men of America. You think that's not possible because what the fuck does the working man know about business? Horseshit! That's what the bosses want you to think."

As Durkin paused to take a drink of water, Garrity sensed something. He looked up and saw a man on the hotel roof throwing something down with a hissing fuse at the end of it. "Dynamite!" he shouted. "Run! Take cover!" The short-fused cluster of dynamite sticks hit the front of the platform and bounced off. Garrity caught it, turned and threw it high above the scattering crowd and down the slope toward the muddy river. It exploded before it hit the ground. There was a bright thunderous flash and the few houses on the far side of the street were blown to bits, showering burning boards and pieces of metal and glass down on what was left of the crowd. Running men, some with their clothes on fire, stumbled over bodies dead or unconscious or screaming in pain. Garrity and Kinnock had been knocked down by the blast of hot air that followed the explosion. Garrity got up and dragged Kinnock to his feet and slapped away sparks that were burning into his clothes. Junk was still raining down through the thick black smoke that covered everything. Kinnock staggered as Garrity let go of him and snatched the light gun from its case. A big bunch of hooded riders were coming in fast from the north end of town. Garrity could see their white hoods and robes through the drifting smoke, and they were firing right and left before they even got close. Garrity jumped up on the platform and knocked the heavy oak table over on its side. Then he got behind it, steadied the light gun and opened fire, raking the bunched up riders and horses with bullets. The union men on the porch cut loose with shotguns, as did the guards at the upstairs windows. Shotguns and rifles joined the chatter of the light gun. Durkin crawled up beside Garrity and opened fire with his pistol. But it was the light gun that did most of the killing. Heavy fire came from the Klansmen, but they were on horseback and not shooting too straight. The horses and riders out in front of the others went down as short bursts from the light gun tore into them. One rider who hadn't been hit kept wheeling his horse, trying to light a stick of dynamite. Garrity gave him a long burst and horse and rider disappeared. The men and horses close to the explosion were knocked down, dead or badly wounded. Behind them the rest of the Klansmen were trying to turn their horses, trying to ride out the way they'd come in. Garrity jumped down from the platform and chased them with bullets, firing most of the bullets left in the light-gun feed box. He had about 100 rounds left, but it wasn't likely that they'd dismount and try to sneak back behind the one-street town or make their way along the slope that went down to the river.

The smoke had drifted away and it was quiet

except for the cries of the wounded. The carbide lamps hadn't been hit and they still threw harsh bright light over the street and the bodies and dead horses lying in it. Garrity set down the light gun and started to shoot wounded horses with his shoulder gun. Durkin and his men started to look at the wounded, and when one of the organizers shot a wounded Klansman in the head, Durkin knocked him down with a savage punch.

"None of that," he told the rest of them. "People in hiding can see you do it and maybe testify later. Take the wounded people into the hotel and put them in beds, leave the fucking Klansmen lay where they are. Fucking crook marshal can decide what to do with them." He spoke in a low growl, but when he finished giving orders, Durkin shouted, "Come out, people! They're gone and won't be back! Nothing to be afraid of! Come on into the hotel and stay till morning if you want!"

Only a handful of people took Durkin up on his offer. The rest had run for home. Durkin went over to where Garrity was still looking at the dead and wounded Klansmen. By his count, they had killed nine Klansmen and wounded eight, not a bad night's work. But he knew it would have gone the other way if the taped cluster of dynamite sticks had exploded where it was dropped. The bastards had been waiting for the explosion that was supposed to have blown the union men and maybe half the crowd to bits.

"What's your count?" Durkin said.

Garrity told him and Durkin said, "Mine's the same. Too bad we couldn't have killed more of the bastards. That Police Maxim is a dandy little gun."

When Garrity said nothing, Durkin went on. "Saw the Police Maxim when I was in England last year.

61

Was down by Hyde Park Corner when a big mob of anarchists started a riot and were threatening to march on Buckingham Palace. Got as far as the Palace and I followed along. Coppers couldn't turn them back with nightsticks so they brought out a Police Maxim and cut loose with it. 'Course England being England, they fired over their heads. No more riot."

Garrity walked away from Durkin without making any comment. The marshal would be back soon since the dynamiting and shooting had stopped. He could picture the fat marshal sweating out there in the dark—that is, unless he'd decided to ride out and try to find some law job in some faraway and quiet town. Garrity didn't think he would because his job must have been pretty soft before the trouble started. And maybe the trouble wouldn't last all that long, and then it would be back to the soft life. Besides, what town would want to hire a shifty-looking lawman with no reputation?

Garrity got to the hotel and asked one of the union men if he'd seen Kinnock. The man said he was lying down on a couch in the lobby. "Not hurt too bad far as I can tell," the man said. "Maybe some concussion. I used to be head orderly in the sick bay, battleship *Farragut*. A mild concussion, I'd say."

Garrity found Kinnock sitting up on the couch. Torrance was holding a glass to his mouth. "Well, he wouldn't take my advice and go home," the lawyer said. "I guess he'll be all right. That fellow Meeker thinks he may have a mild concussion. If that worthless marshal doesn't get back soon, I'd put him in the buckboard, fix him up with cushions and take him home."

"Let him rest for a bit," Garrity said, thinking he'd like to hear what the marshal had to say.

Durkin was sitting in a rocker when he went out to the porch. The bodies of the dead Klansmen were sprawled under the glaring lights. A dead horse lay on top of one of them. Two badly wounded Klansmen had just died, Durkin told him. "Some of the others are begging for water. I wouldn't give them the steam off my piss. I got fourteen wounded men in there"—Durkin meant the hotel—"and no doctor. That lawyer sent a rider to fetch an old retired doctor who lives ten miles out in the county. Till he gets here, one of my men, Meeker, is doing what he can."

"I talked to Meeker," Garrity said.

Torrance came out, nodded to Durkin and said to Garrity, "He's gone back to sleep. I made him drink a glass of beer and it made him sleepy." Torrance made a clucking sound with his tongue. "Will wonders never cease!"

"I see them," Garrity said. The marshal and his deputies were riding up from the south end of town. Some man was walking alongside them, talking excitedly in a high-pitched voice. The three men rode up to the platform and dismounted. Another look at the dead and wounded night-riders made the marshal's jowly face sag even more. Garrity, Durkin and the lawyer came down from the porch.

"What happened here, Torrance?" The marshal had to hock and spit before he could talk again. Then he told the talky man to shut up and go the hell home.

"What happened is what you see," the lawyer said calmly. "Some Klansmen tossed a bunch of dynamite down from the roof of the hotel. A big bunch of sticks taped together, a real short fuse. It was meant for Mr. Durkin and his men, but it would have killed half the crowd if it had landed right. It bounced off the platform. Mr. Garrity caught it and threw it away far as he could. It blew up beyond the far side of the street, knocked down houses, killed five men, wounded fourteen. And that, Marshal, is what happened. May I inquire as to where you and your two stalwarts were at the time?"

The marshal tried to outstare the feisty little lawyer and failed. "We got word Clem Tobey was holed up in the old Jeans place back a mile from the South Road. I went to take a look. He wasn't there."

Torrance smiled. "Clem Tobey is a badman famous in three counties. Ever hear of him, Mr. Garrity? Of course you haven't. Clem is about as dangerous as my Aunt Matilda."

"Get on with it, Torrance," the marshal said, trying to ignore the lawyer's sarcasm. It wasn't easy. "Who killed and wounded all these men?"

"I suppose you could call them men," the lawyer said. "The answer is everybody that could fire a gun killed them. I could have killed some of them." The lawyer took an old Colt Peacemaker from under his coat. "I fired off the whole six. I killed them. Garrity killed them. Durkin and his men killed them. I'm not rightly sure, but I think I saw the Widow Gruber letting fly with a blunderbuss."

"You're not funny."

"Probably not. What's funny is you, Marshal. I know there's a big fifty-dollar-reward notice out on Clem, but is that any reason to leave this town unprotected?"

The marshal gave up on Torrance and turned to Garrity. "You tell it."

"The dynamite was the signal for the Klan to ride in. They heard the explosion and thought it would be fish in a barrel. We cut loose with everything we had. I couldn't see the surprised look on their faces—they had hoods on."

Torrance was back to needling the marshal. "I think you could say we acted in self-defense. Or are you going to charge us with shooting down a bunch of poor, harmless Klansmen out for a ride on a pleasant summer night?"

"Where's Kinnock?" the marshal said.

"Kinnock killed nobody," Garrity said. "He was knocked out when the blast knocked him down and he hit his head. He's resting in the hotel."

They all turned when a black man came out of the shadows and walked over to where they were. Garrity knew he'd never seen him before. He was wearing the bib overalls of a farmer. Sweat ran down his coal-black face and he was shaking all over.

The marshal knew him. "What you want, Lucky?"

"I saw the whole thing," the black man said, starting slow, but beginning to babble as he went on. "I live here all my life an' knows ev'body. Some of dem Kans dat got away. I knows some of dem too. One of dem, Billy Whittaker, had dat long gun of his buckle on outside his robe. I knows him. I can testify." A strong smell of whiskey came from the black man called Lucky.

The marshal pushed him hard and he fell. He was still lying there, wild eyed, when the marshal reached for his gun.

"Let him be," Garrity said.

Chapter Five

The marshal turned slowly and looked at his deputies before he spoke to Garrity. Wakely and Spoon had their hands close to their guns. Wakely looked as if he had more nerve than Spoon, but they'd both draw if the marshal did.

"You want to take on the three of us?" the marshal said to Garrity. "You think you're that good, do you?"

Durkin cut in, saying, "It won't be just Garrity. You got to take me into account."

"And me," the lawyer added. "I'm no great shot, but it would be hard to miss with you standing so close. Get out of here, Lucky. Be gone, I say."

Lucky got to his feet and staggered away until he was lost in darkness. It was quiet except for the moaning of the wounded Klansmen. Garrity figured to kill the marshal if it came to killing. He wondered how good Durkin was with a gun. No doubt he'd used guns in his time, but his gun was stuck in his belt inside his coat and he might not get it out fast enough. The lawyer was just talking. On the other hand, Spoon and Wakely looked as if they might be fast enough.

"You were about to kill an unarmed man, Marshal," Garrity said. "Couldn't let you do that. Why would you want to kill a poor old drunken black man?"

The marshal just stared at Garrity.

"The marshal wanted to kill him because he identified Billy Whittaker," the lawyer said. "Lucky said he could identify some of the others, not that a West Texas court would take a black man's word. But maybe the court will believe us."

"What do you want to do, Marshal?" Garrity said. "You want a shootout or you want to do your job? You got wounded Klansmen to look after and then lock up."

The night wind was drying the sweat on the marshal's face and Garrity could see he was glad the moment had passed and he was still alive. Only Wakely still had his hand close to his gun. Trouble could still come from Wakely.

The best the marshal could do was to take his time about answering. Finally he said, "This isn't over, Garrity, but there's been too much killing for one night. Come up against me one more time and you won't walk away from it. You may be a gunslick, but I can deputize ten men if it takes that many to put you down."

Garrity wanted to laugh, but he didn't doubt that the marshal could round up 20 men without much trouble. Twenty Klansmen without their bed sheets. That would be up to Pig Meat Mayfield, the man who preferred pork chops to porterhouse. Let them try.

"We'll be leaving now, Marshal," he said. "Kinnock's banged up and ought to be put to bed. You want signed statements, we'll do it tomorrow, any time you say. Tonight you'll be busy clearing the street of that trash."

Kinnock came out while he was talking. Two of Durkin's shotgun guards were behind him. A third union man, without a shotgun, was holding Kinnock up. Garrity took over and they started for the buckboard, the lawyer following along with cushions. Durkin called from the porch, "Don't worry about getting backshot, Garrity. You got two sawed-offs watching over you, and there's me. Take good care of his lordship. I'll be calling on him soon as he gets well."

While they were settling Kinnock in the buckboard, Garrity said, "You think Barrows will lock up those bastards?"

"I don't know. There were eight wounded. Durkin's man killed one. Two died. That leaves five. I wouldn't be at all surprised if they expired during the night. Yes, sir," Torrance said.

"Barrows would do a thing like that?"

"Mayfield would. Barrows will kill them if Mayfield says so. He'll leave it to the deputies."

"But if he doesn't kill them and they come to trial, not much chance of a conviction, you think?"

"That's what I think. Bringing them to trial would be up to the county prosecutor. He's new in the job, so it's hard to say what he'd do. But I can tell you right now, if they do stand trial for murder, they'll get off. No Lawton County jury will vote to convict. But I'm betting they'll never see the sun come up. If they're held they'll have to be taken to the county jail hospital. One of them might talk, put a name to every member of the Klan, drag Mayfield and the marshal into it. It would be hard to sweep that under the rug. You better get going. One last thing: if you see that dumb, drunken Lucky sleeping by the road or in the middle of it for that matter, rouse him up and send him on his way. Better still, tell him to get the hell out of this county. Of all the dumb things to do, talking to Barrows like that. If Barrows doesn't tell the Klan, Wakely will. When will I be seeing you?"

"Tomorrow. Sometime tomorrow. You'll be all right after what happened tonight?"

"I'm always all right," the lawyer said. "They wouldn't dare kill me. My father was a hero of the Sam Houston War. He was a lawyer, a judge and a senator when Texas was a republic. He built the first house in this town in 1855. Good night, Garrity."

With the gun case at his feet, Garrity drove slowly for fear of waking Kinnock, who lay back with cushions to keep him steady, a blanket to keep him warm. Torrance said he'd send the old doctor out in the morning.

Garrity was glad to get away from the stink of blood, dynamite and the loosed shit of dying men. There was no sign of Lucky or the Klan or anybody. Torrance said to drive five miles until he reached the branch road that went three miles to the Kinnock ranch. Kinnock woke up before they got to the turnoff. He sat up straight, knocking one of the cushions off the buckboard. He said, "Garrity!"

"Right here," Garrity said. "You're on your way home. Go back to sleep. Must have been a rock under the dirt. You took a bad rap on the head.

Doctor will be out in the morning. How're you feeling?"

"I have a thundering great headache. I don't remember being knocked down by the blast, but I do remember when you dragged me to my feet. I fell a second time."

"I had to let go of you. They were coming in, firing in all directions." Garrity gave him the casualty figures for both sides, not wanting to drag through it with questions and answers. Kinnock sat up straight when he was told that Durkin and his shotgunners had covered them when then they left town.

"With me dead there would be nothing left to organize," Kinnock said. "Or he wants to keep me alive because he thinks I'm an easier mark than Mayfield would be."

"That could be. All I'm saying is, he didn't run and hide when the shooting started, so he isn't all mouth. I'm not asking you to like him—I don't like him—but he can't be as bad as Pig Meat Mayfield."

"That remains to be seen," Kinnock said.

They reached the branch road and not much later the gate to Kinnock's ranch. It was more a boundary marker than a gate: two stout poles about 15 feet high with a cross flatboard that had Kinnock painted on it in large black letters. No fence ran away on either side of it. Garrity figured there would be smaller fenced areas inside the ranch boundary line. There was no guard at the gate. No point in keeping guard when there was so much unfenced country to cross. Garrity saw lights after he'd driven a mile from the gate.

A long low log ranchhouse protected by windbreak trees looked solid in the moonlight. There was a horse corral at one end of it, two bunkhouses not far away. A windmill creaked in the darkness. A dog barked and the door of the house opened and a burly man came out and closed the door behind him. He moved fast, but Garrity saw he was holding a rifle or shotgun.

"Is that you, Kinnock?" a Scots-accented voice called out.

Kinnock was too weak to do much shouting, so Garrity shouted, "Kinnock's here but he's been hurt a bit. My name is Garrity. Maybe Kinnock told you I was coming. Are you Murdo?"

No answer came right away, then the burly man suddenly appeared at the other side of the buckboard. "I'm Murdo and I'm right behind you with a shotgun pointing at your head. Aye, it's Kinnock sure enough. Can ye talk, Kinnock?"

Kinnock roused himself. "I hear you, Murdo. I took a bang on the head. Garrity's all right, a friend."

Murdo handed the double-barreled shotgun to Garrity before he helped Kinnock into the house. He laid Kinnock on a sofa, but Kinnock insisted on sitting up.

Kinnock told Murdo what he remembered and Garrity filled in the rest. Murdo wasn't tall, but he was built like a barrel. He wore a rough tweed suit, a round stiff-brimmed hat, laced boots with thick soles. A thick, short gray beard covered most of his face like a mask. Above the beard his eyes were small and blue and cold. Instead of a gunbelt he wore a canvas belt studded with shotgun shells.

"You better get him to bed," Garrity said. "Doctor will be out in the morning."

Murdo came back five minutes later and asked Garrity if he wanted a drink. Garrity said no thanks and Murdo sat down facing him. Murdo wasn't a young man, but he looked very rough, a man with a quick temper and big hairy fists to back it up.

71

"Kinnock often works late, but not this late," Murdo said in a growl that Garrity decided was the only way he spoke. Coming from the barrel chest, from behind the beard, it sounded natural. "I was all set to round up a bunch of the boys and ride into town to look for him."

The big main room of the house was plainly furnished but comfortable. There were bookcases and framed maps of Scotland and Texas and other places, colorful rugs scattered on the sanded floor. A log fire was burning in the rough stone fireplace. Bottles of Scotch and bourbon stood on a sideboard.

"Just as well you didn't," Garrity said. "The marshal would say you were out nightriding like the Klan."

"Aye, I suppose he would, the dirty hypocrite. I don't know how that feelthy crook can face himself in the mirror when he shaves. But no doubt he's well paid for his double-dealing."

"No doubt," Garrity said. "I get the feeling that he'd rather not be a part of this, but he's afraid of Mayfield. I guess most people are afraid of Mayfield."

"So they are," Murdo said. "I'm not and neither is Kinnock or that little lawyer. That makes three of us, and you, of course. The four brave men of Lawton County. How brave do ye feel, Garrity?"

"I never feel brave till the danger's past."

Murdo's big laugh filled the room; then he remembered that Kinnock was sleeping not far away. "Och aye, it's no laughing matter, any of it. Speaking of brav'ry, there's only one thing I'm afraid of and that's the knife. The thought of cold steel gives me the wullies."

"We're all afraid of something, Murdo." Garrity

paused to think back on it. "I'm afraid of being hanged. I came close to it some years back."

"And I got a knife in the guts that kept me in bed for three months. Damn wound festered inside and I was shitting green and spitting green. Doctor that finally cut me open and cured me said I was a case for the medical books. The knife had penetrated my guts and I had what he called perrytownisis ... you'd think I'd remember how to say it right."

"Peritonitis," Garrity said.

"That's what was trying to kill me," Murdo said. "All the other doctors had given up on me. Then this young doctor that was passing through, looking for a town to hang his shingle, took a chance. Was honest about it, said I'd prob'ly die during the operation. Get to it, says I. I won't come back and haunt you if I do die. Operated on me right there in the kitchen of my own little house. Nervy young woman that helped him, the owner's daughter, told me later the young doc cut me open, hung my intestines over the back of a kitchen chair and cut off I don't know how many feet was all rotted and diseased. Took me months to recover, but I did."

Garrity didn't know what to say to his grisly story. All he could think to say was, "I always heard British doctors were pretty good."

Murdo did his best to laugh quietly. "British doctors my arse. This happened three days ride south of Laramie. Oh sure, you were thinking I'm an old retainer of the Kinnock family and I been pulling my forelock and trotting ten paces behind the laird since I was a boy. Admit it, man, that's what you had me pegged for."

"Sort of. I don't know about pulling the forelock."

That time Murdo didn't laugh. He took off his peculiar-looking hat to display a completely bald head with a number of scars on it. "Tell the truth, man, d'ye think I look like an old retainer?"

"No," Garrity said. "I sure wouldn't want you for a butler."

"Nor would I work for you had you need of such a useless thing, and I have no use for them that has. I left Scotland when I was just a lad and the landlord drove my family off the land to make grazing room for sheep. Ye see, in those days sheep were better value than human beings. That was forty-five years ago and they treated us as bad as the Irish. Highland people we were. Only difference between us and the Irish was the Irish never did take it lying down and still haven't. The bloody rotten landlord got us passage to Canada, but there the family split up and I wandered south. I been working on ranches all my life."

Garrity said nothing because he could tell Murdo wasn't finished yet. "You're wondering how with my hate for the nobility I come to be manager for Kinnock. Well, sir, I happened to be in these parts and heard Kinnock was looking for a manager. I was of no mind to work for nobility, but then I heard good things about him and I needed a job so I thought what the hell I might as well see what he's like. That was close on two years ago and I've never regretted it. The man has treated me fair and square, no cowshit, no airs and graces, no putting on the dog. It was Kinnock and Murdo right from the start. Used to be I was Mr. Murdo on every ranch I managed. Now the greenest kid on the place calls me Murdo because they call the boss Kinnock. I'd do anything for that man. It's a bloody shame what they're trying to do to him. I'm for putting the fear of God into Mayfield and Durkin, but Kinnock won't hear of it. What d'ye think, Garrity?"

"I don't know," Garrity said, not quite sure how he should take the dangerous bear of a man. Anything he said about Kinnock might be taken the wrong way. "I haven't been here twenty-four hours yet and we've argued about what he should do. I'm for putting Mayfield where the dogs won't bite him. I don't know about Durkin."

Murdo scratched his stubbly beard. "Aye, Mayfield is the main enemy. Durkin looks like he's had too hard a life, but Mayfield was born bad. Bad seed went into the making of that man. Ye'd have to go a far piece to find a man as bad as he is. A shame he doesn't fall down a well or get gored by a bull."

Garrity thought Murdo gave him a sly look when he said, " 'Course t'would be better if he bet he could stop a bullet with his forehead."

"And lost the bet," Garrity said. "Can we talk straight, Murdo?"

"Straight as a carpenter's level is how I like to talk. I think I could kill Mayfield. In my forty-five years in the West I've killed my share of men—Indians, rustlers and so forth. But I'm handicapped when it comes to killing a lump of shit like Mayfield. I never said a word about it to Kinnock, but he warned me off just the same. I have to respect his wishes, don't you see?"

All Garrity did was nod.

"You, on the other hand, are under no such handicap," Murdo went on. I know you didn't come here to tell Mayfield what a bad lad he is. If ye don't mind a straight question, what d'ye plan to do?"

"I don't know. The reason I'm here is to help Kinnock get out from under this, but it's like talking to the wall talking to him. He won't take the war to Mayfield, the only way to do it, and at the same time he seems to have no idea how to stop the son of a bitch. If he's counting on the law to help him he can forget it. This isn't Scotland."

"Tisn't even Canada," Murdo said. "What wouldn't I give for a platoon of redcoats?"

Redcoats my ass! Garrity thought. He liked Murdo well enough, what he could see of him, but he was a bit of a windbag. And there was no guarantee that he wouldn't report their whole conversation to Kinnock in the morning. Maybe he was an old retainer after all, or had become one late in life. Garrity didn't think he'd said anything that would get Kinnock's back up. He needed the ranch to store his weapons and ammunition, especially the Motor Scout.

"By the way," Murdo said, watching him closely, "those crates the teamsters brought out yesterday, they're in a safe place in the barn, but I'm thinking they'd better be moved where there's less danger of fire. The Klan could decide to ride in here in the dead of night. Your goods—"

"They're weapons, things I'll be using if I get a chance." Garrity didn't explain what they were. Time enough for that when he got to know Murdo better. A loyal windbag was still a windbag. He might have a wife or a woman who talked too much. He had said nothing about a wife and Garrity hadn't asked.

"I'll have the crates moved to the stone building we keep our dynamite in. Part of the wall will have to be knocked out to get the biggest crate in. Then it can be rebuilt and a wider door made. I'll post a guard at night."

"Maybe we'd better leave them where they are," Garrity said. "Knocking out walls and posting guards would get too much attention. Men talk meaning no harm and Mayfield could have a spy among the hands."

Because of the beard there was no way of knowing if Murdo got red in the face. His big ears got red and he said angrily, "There's no spy on the ranch. I hired every last man myself. I don't even let the foreman do the hiring. Other managers do, not me. I'm a good judge of men, laddie."

Garrity was pushing 40 and no one had ever called him laddie before. "All spies aren't shifty eyed, but I'll take your word for it. Even so, we'll leave the weapons where they are. If the Klan can burn the barn they can burn the house and run off the horses. Do you post a night guard?"

"Aye, there's two men watching the place at night. Kinnock says that's enough."

"It's not enough. Post more night guards here and between here and the gate. They can come cross country, but why ride around in the hills when there's a good undefended road right to your doorstep. They must know that. It's the first thing Mayfield would want to know. It's the first thing I'd want to know."

Murdo's ears got red again. "You're not telling me anything I don't know. D'ye think I'm a greenhorn straight off the boat? I was shooting and hanging nightriding rustlers before you were old enough to raise a gun. What you're saying ought to be done, but how am I going to do it if Kinnock says no?"

"Then do it without him knowing, for his own good. Would he fire you if he found out?"

"He might. He's a fair man, but doesn't like to be crossed." Garrity sensed uneasiness in Murdo's answer. He had found a top job late in life, and if Kinnock sent him packing he'd be hard set to find another job as good. Kinnock's ranch was set up like many big ranches: a foreman ran the ranch, a manager oversaw everything. A manager, with so

many men under him, was like a little king. In all
but the really big decisions his word was law. Murdo
wouldn't want to lose all that.

"The foreman would be sure to tell him," Murdo
said. "Bugger wants my job and he could see that
as a way to get it. But he'd be no good as a manager. The man is next to illeeterate, is all he can do
to struggle through the newspaper. I taught myself
bookkeeping that time I was laid up with the bad
gut. I keep no clerk. I keep the books myself."

"Then Kinnock would hardly fire you."

Murdo laughed his growly laugh. "Ah, ye don't
have to soft-soap me, Garrity. I'll post the guards
as you suggest. When the real bad trouble comes,
and it surely will, Kinnock will be glad I did. I'll
be out checking the guards at least twice a night.
They'll never know what time to expect me, and that
should keep them from dozing off. And what, might
I ask, will you be doing?"

Garrity had no ready answer for that. "Looking
around," he said. "Getting set. I can't say I have a
plan because I don't."

"Well, that's honest."

"How are you fixed for weapons?"

"Not as good as I'd like us to be. Most of the boys
own pistols. As for rifles, not too many own rifles. I
mean, there's more than enough rifles and ammunition for the guards. But for a big fight or a long
war we're not well equipped. No rifles for sale in
town. Somebody bought them all up. Same thing
in Amarillo. I'm going to have to order them from
a long way off."

"I'll get you rifles faster than that, and nobody will
stop them from getting through."

Murdo stood up when Kinnock called out in his
sleep. "I'd better look in on him. If you're hungry

there's loads of food in the kitchen. Cold roast beef, potato salad, apple pie."

"I'll eat in the morning," Garrity said.

"Then I'll show you where you bunk," Murdo said. "I think I'll sleep with my clothes on this night. I doubt if the Klan will pay us a visit, but you never know. Mayfield may figure we won't be on guard for them."

Garrity agreed and decided to sleep with the light gun on the floor beside his bed.

Chapter Six

Garrity was eating breakfast when Torrance arrived about eight the next morning. Kinnock was still in bed. Murdo brought the lawyer into the kitchen, saying, "Everybody must know Barrows and his deputies did it."

"They know no such thing," Torrance said. "Well, it happened more or less like I said." That was said to Garrity. "On about four this morning a bunch of men, all masked, broke into the jail, overpowered Barrows and his deputies and hung the prisoners from the ceiling beams. That's Barrows's story and he's sticking to it."

The lawyer was unshaven and looked as if he hadn't been to bed. "Ten men did the lynching, according to Barrows. He says he heard more men outside. Maybe there were that many men, but Barrows let them in."

Garrity poured coffee for Torrance, who lifted the cup with an unsteady hand. That wasn't like Torrance. The little lawyer was good and rattled. "Barrows is accusing you, Garrity. He says he's pretty sure he recognized you in spite of the mask, the different clothes you wore, and the big floppy hat. That's a crafty touch. A man would have to be a fool to lead a lynching in town clothes."

Garrity speared the last of his fried ham. He had cooked his own breakfast because Kinnock's black cook was out of action with serious grease burns.

"Did he identify Kinnock?" Garrity asked.

"No. But he says he knows Kinnock was behind it," the lawyer said. "And there's nobody to contradict him. Naturally, his deputies go along with everything he says. Wakely was wearing his gloves when I went to the jail. I think maybe he's got rope burns on one hand. He favored it a bit. But that's neither here nor there. They have their story and won't budge from it. It hasn't even been challenged."

"Is Barrows ready to bring charges against me?" Garrity asked, thinking he'd rather be shot dead than have a posse bring him in.

"I can't rightly say. The impression I got is that he's trying to get things stirred up and keep them stirred. The town was full of Klansmen and others when I left this morning. Nothing like this ever happened before in Lawton, at least not to white men. It must have been horrible, to be dragged out and lynched by men you'd known all your life. They must have been begging for mercy, shitting their pants when they were hauled up. Not even a clean drop—they choked to death. Ugly as sin."

Garrity didn't give a damn if the lynched men had pissed their way to perdition, but he knew what the lawyer meant. No matter what the truth was, it was home folks against foreigners, and to West Texans he was as much a foreigner as Kinnock and Murdo. A man from the next state was a foreigner.

"Any sign of Mayfield?" Garrity asked.

"No. But the saloon was doing land office business, so Mayfield must have spread a little money around. I heard your friend Whittaker yelling as I passed by. No way to be sure, but he could have led the lynch party. Billy likes to inflict pain on others. Friend or enemy, it doesn't matter."

Kinnock came into the kitchen wearing a red undershirt, pants and socks. He showed no surprise at seeing Torrance there. Garrity poured coffee for him.

Torrance told him about the lynching and why the doctor hadn't come with him. "He's old and afraid and just wants to live out his years. The state gives him some kind of medical officer pension, a pittance, but he needs it. Mayfield could have it stopped."

Kinnock felt his head and winced. "I don't need a doctor. It hurts, but I'm all right. I've got to get started for the plant."

Torrance looked alarmed. "I don't know if I'd do that, Kinnock. There's nothing but trouble in town. Why not wait for things to calm down?"

"And what will happen to the plant if I don't show up there? If Mayfield can use Barrows to keep me away from my own plant, I might as well give up."

Garrity knew Kinnock was right. If the Klansmen in town, fired up by Mayfield's whiskey money, decided to burn the plant, nothing much would happen. They would burn the plant and disappear.

"Kinnock's right," Garrity said. "He has to make an appearance and never mind what happened at the jail. I'll go with him and I'll take the machine gun. If they're ready to face that, fine by me. Look, Kinnock, I'm not looking to kill another bunch of Klansmen, but we have to be ready for them."

Kinnock nodded. "Very well."

"I'll go with ye," Murdo said.

Kinnock shook his head. "Stay here, Murdo, and hold the fort. Two men or ten men won't make that much difference. Garrity has the machine gun, but they have the numbers. Of course, they won't be so eager to face it close up. We'll just have to wait and see what they do. Mr. Torrance, I don't think you should be seen with us."

The lawyer shrugged. "Doesn't make any difference. They know where I went by now."

Kinnock pulled on his boots. "Perhaps you would like to stay here for a while?"

"Hide here, you mean?"

"Keep out of harm's way is what I mean."

Torrance smiled. "The same as you're doing?"

"I have to show myself in Lawton," Kinnock said. "You don't, not for a few days, perhaps a week."

Torrance got up without finishing his coffee. "Garrity is my client and may have to face a more serious charge, namely premeditated murder. If he's charged, I have to make sure he's still alive when his case comes up."

Kinnock took his shirt and coat from Murdo and put them on. "All right, you're Garrity's lawyer. That doesn't mean you have to ride in with us."

Torrance turned toward the door. "I insist. I'm nervous for the first time since this trouble started. I used to think nobody would ever kill me, but now

I'm not so sure. Even so, I might lose my nerve completely if I holed up here. Courage may come easily to you, but not to me. I have to work at it."

Garrity rode one of Kinnock's geldings, Torrance an elderly brown mare that would be hard set to break into a gallop. Kinnock drove his buckboard with a double-barreled shotgun on the seat beside him. They would have made better time if the lawyer's horse hadn't been so old. The light gun was in the back of the buckboard, covered by a blanket. Two linked belts of 300 rounds were linked and loaded and ready to fire. The gun case was open so he could get at the gun in a hurry.

Garrity kept watching for smoke as they got closer to Lawton. Smoke could only mean that the packing plant had been set on fire, but the sky remained clear all the way to town. They got to the railroad depot and Garrity sent a coded message to Col. Pritchett in New York, asking him to ship 200 Winchester rifles and 25,000 rounds of ammunition by the fastest means possible, and they were to be sent to Amarillo, not to Lawton. Garrity didn't know if the colonel would send the rifles from New York or if he knew an arms dealer closer to West Texas. One way or another, the rifles would be shipped. Anything to keep Maxim on Victoria's good side.

To get to the packing plant from the depot they had to ride through town. This was the hardest part because, small though the town was, it had enough rooftops to hide a dozen snipers. Garrity didn't want to ride with the light gun in one hand, so he rode right behind the buckboard. There were more people in town than there had been the day before. Nothing like mass murder to bring out the curious.

Durkin and one of his men were on the porch of

the hotel. The platform was gone. "Hold up there a minute," Durkin called out. Garrity turned his horse toward the porch. Two men with sawed-offs came and stood in the doorway.

"Bad doings last night, early this morning," Durkin said. "Five Klan prisoners got lynched by parties unknown. Good riddance and so forth, but that crooked fucking marshal is measuring me and my men for striped suits."

"Same here," Garrity said. "Says he's next to dead certain the boss lyncher was me."

"Was he?"

"No. Were you?"

Durkin's laugh had no humor in it. "Not my style. Too many of my people have been lynched, tarred and feathered, had their backs broken for me to go in for that kind of shit. Watch yourself, Garrity. I figure the marshal wants you more than he wants me."

They were close to the Good Times saloon when a lookout darted inside. Billy Whittaker came out with about 20 men behind him, all boozed up and ready for trouble. Whittaker was still wearing a sling, but he had exchanged the marshal's makeshift sling for a colorful silk scarf knotted in a bow at the shoulder. The marshal or his deputies were nowhere in sight.

Whittaker and the others got down off the porch and blocked the street. Kinnock reined in and gave Garrity a quick look. "Make way," he said. "You're blocking the public street."

"No, we're not, your stinking lordship. It's a public street and we're holding a public meeting in it. If Durkin and his tramps can do it, so can we. You're not thinking of running us down, are you? Better turn back before somebody gets hurt. Hey, Garrity, why are you hanging back there? You hiding behind this Scotsman's kilts?"

Garrity was close enough to the light gun to grab it out of the case, but decided he'd handle the situation with the shoulder-holstered Colt .45. Maybe he could wipe out most of the Lawton County Klan with the light gun. He figured most of them were there, drunk or half-drunk, ready to back Whittaker's play. But when the smoke cleared, he'd be dead and so would Kinnock and Torrance. He knew Torrance was no hand with a gun and he doubted if Kinnock had ever shot at a man in his life. So, finally, it would be his gun against twenty-one.

"Hey, Garrity!" Whittaker shouted again. "You ever get your hand under the Scotsman's kilt? Is it true you don't like women?"

Garrity dismounted and tied his horse to the endgate of the buckboard. Then he walked forward to face Whittaker. If he could make Whittaker back off, the rest might follow. Sometimes it worked, sometimes it didn't. His coat was open and the short-barreled Sheriff's Model Colt .45 rested lightly in the greased holster. He had put another film of grease on the inside of the holster just hours earlier.

Whittaker swayed on his feet, but Garrity didn't think he was as drunk as he was letting on. Garrity walked up close and he was surprised enough to back off a little. Now they were no more than five feet apart. Whittaker's long-barreled pistol was good for distance shooting, not so good up close, where a gun like that tended to be unwieldly.

"I like women fine," Garrity said in a very loud voice. "But I don't try to castrate their husbands to get them. If I want a woman I don't get her drawers down by cutting off her husband's balls. You got two years in prison for that. You should have got twenty, you dumb, vicious, sneaking son of a bitch." Garrity's voice was so loud it could be heard from one end of the street to the other. "I don't know what the rest of you men are like, but you can't be like this ball-cutting bastard. It's a wonder to me you'd be seen in public with him, let alone drink with him."

Whittaker just gaped at him. He hadn't ever run into someone like Garrity. A murmur ran through the gang of Klansmen behind him and people on the single boardwalk were talking in whispers.

"Draw if you have a mind to draw," Garrity shouted in Whittaker's face. "If not, let us through. The rest of you keep out of it. This is between the ball-cutter and me. I'll bet you enjoyed handling that man's cock and balls, Whittaker."

Whittaker hesitated and Garrity roared, "Get the hell out of our way! You wear your gun like you think you're fast. Show us how fast. You have the advantage. That should suit you. Show us, pigface!"

Whittaker's hand streaked for his gun, but Garrity's .45 was out and cocked and pointing at his face before his pistol cleared leather. Sweat ran down Whittaker's face as he tried not to look into the bore of the stubby pistol that could end his life with a squeeze of the trigger. Garrity wanted to pistol-whip the son of a bitch, but decided that would be a mistake. These shit-kicking backcountry Klansmen had their own code and they might not hold still while one of their number was bloodied with a pistol barrel. They might accept the killing of Whittaker—he would be beaten in a fair fight—but messing up his face might start them shooting.

"Take your gun out with your left hand," Garrity ordered. "Kick out the loads and put the gun back in your holster. Then walk away from here. Run if you like. Run to Pig Meat and tell him how brave you were today. Do what I tell you, Whittaker."

Whittaker prodded the shells out of the loading gate and reholstered his shiny gunfighter's gun. His thin face was tight with shame and anger.

"Let's go, boys," he said. "Drinks're on me."

"Hold up a minute," Garrity said, taking a $50 Mexican gold piece from his pocket. He held the coin between thumb and forefinger so the sun hit it. They knew what it was. "I'll bet Mayfield gave good old Billy nothing but rotgut money. This'll buy better than that."

Garrity flipped the coin to the side of the street, where it was swallowed by the fine, drifted dust. Nobody scrambled to dig it up, but he knew that would happen as soon as they passed. Whittaker was heading in the direction of the saloon. The mob of Klansmen let the buckboard pass through. Garrity mounted up and followed behind, still not sure that Whittaker wouldn't grab somebody's gun and open fire.

The Klansmen were fighting for the gold piece by the time Garrity and the others reached Torrance's office. "That was the damnedest thing I ever saw," the little lawyer said. "Were you as mad as you sounded or just playacting?"

"A little of both," Garrity said. "Keeping them off balance sometimes works. And sometimes trying to do it can get you killed."

"The fifty-dollar gold piece?"

"I figured it would keep them busy. For most of them fifty dollars is two months' wages. You sure you'll be all right, Mr. Torrance?"

"Don't start that again." The lawyer hitched his horse and headed for the stairs. He turned before he started up. "You got the better of Billy Whittaker twice in two days. Next time he'll try to shoot you in the back."

"I know he'll try, Mr. Torrance."

"Don't downplay him too much. He's a bad bastard and that's no word of a lie."

Garrity and Kinnock went on to the plant. Kinnock acted as general manager, but had three foremen for separate sections. One of them, a big rough Irishman called Kinsella, reported that 200 cowhides had been destroyed by acid during the night and a conveyor belt badly damaged. Kinsella said it would take most of the day to repair the conveyor belt. Until then the sides of beef in that section would have to be carried or moved on hand trucks.

"It'll slow us up a good bit," Kinsella said.

"Do the best you can," Kinnock said.

Later, sitting in the office, Kinnock said, "Well, the plant still stands in spite of the damage. The hides are a fairly profitable sideline, but the company can stand the loss. Damage to the machinery is something else again. Fortunately, we have the parts to repair the damage, but if it happens again we'll have to send to Omaha, and it will cost a great deal of money, much more than usual. A group of major packers are pressuring the equipment companies not to sell to me or the few other independents. Or if they do sell the prices should be so high that no one can afford to pay them. In a way it's like your rifles."

"We'll get the rifles," Garrity said. "If I ask Col. Pritchett to send the rifles it'll be done. Nobody puts pressure on the colonel."

Kinnock looked at Garrity. "And nobody puts pressure on you. I'm afraid too many people put pressure on me."

"You don't have to let them."

"Easier said than done. I suppose you don't think I fit in here, this rough country without much law. Some of the earlier British cattle barons were quite rough and ready, or so I'm told. Ex-officers, a lot of them, as ready to hang a rustler or fight off Indians as they were to drink their sundown brandy and water. Don't tell me you haven't wondered what brought me to this place."

"Now and then."

"It's a little silly, of course, but as a boy my imagination was fired by the very word Texas. Boys' book stuff. The Alamo. The Texas Rangers. The Kiowas and Comanches, all the rest of it. When the first British started leaving for Texas and other parts of the West, I longed to go with them. That was fifteen years ago and I was fifteen. I ran away and got as far as Liverpool, hoping to stowaway on some boat sailing for Galveston or New Orleans, any Southern port. My father sent men after me and they brought me back. When I tried again, he sent me to the strictest school in Scotland, more like a prison than a school. When I was eighteen I was shunted into the Scots Guards as a second lieutenant. Much to my father's annoyance, I was always somewhere else when there was heroic fighting to be done. The day I was informed of my father's death I resigned from the army. As his only son I got all his land and money. That was a little over two years ago."

"You've built up a lot in two years, but why did you settle here? Far as I can see, it doesn't have one damn thing to recommend it. You couldn't have come here for the scenery. There is none, nothing but wind and dust."

"You're wrong there, Garrity. It's beautiful country in its way. But I came here because land was cheaper here, and West Texas seemed closer to the old Texas frontier. It still is. I know it's 1890 and the frontier is pretty much gone, but even so West Texas still has the space and freedom I used to dream about as a lad."

West Texas will knock the dreams out of you, Garrity thought. It had a way of doing that. What he'd just heard was a long speech for Kinnock, a man who guarded his emotions and the things he said.

Kinnock didn't say anything for a while. "I've been thinking," he said. "About those rifles, do you think you—we—need so many?"

"Probably not."

"Then why so many?"

"To let Mayfield know you have powerful friends. The message to the colonel was sent in code so even the telegrapher didn't know what it said. But the colonel's name and address had to be in plain English. I don't know if the telegraphers give information to Mayfield. Like as not they do. If they do, then he'll know I sent a message to the Maxim Arms Company and he'll be checking on who the colonel is. He'll know it means guns or something to help you fight a war."

"I don't want to fight a war."

"But you will if it's forced on you. That dynamite bomb wasn't meant to give you a headache."

"That bomb wasn't meant for me," Kinnock said.

Garrity managed to keep his temper reined in because getting mad at Kinnock didn't accomplish anything. "It was meant for Durkin and his men, but you were in the front row and, come to think of it, so was I. Forget about me. You'd have been blown to bits if that bomb had landed right. That's the way it is with bombs, Kinnock: they don't pick and choose."

"No need for sarcasm," Kinnock said stiffly. "But to get back to these rifles, if Mayfield knows you're expecting some kind of arms shipment—perhaps men as well as rifles—what's to stop him from sending his thugs to attack the train? Or to attack it when it reaches the Lawton depot?"

"We'll take the rifles off the train when it's halfway to Lawton and take them to the ranch in wagons. By the time Mayfield hears about it, it'll be too late. Some of the rifles can be used to defend the plant. You've got to face up to this trouble, Kinnock."

Kinnock gave out with a breathy sigh. "I'm trying to. The hell of it is all I wanted was to start a business, to provide employment, to harm no one. I don't think I'm a coward, but I hate the thought of killing other men no matter how misguided."

Misguided—now there was a word, Garrity thought. In his time he'd heard the Klan called many things, but never misguided.

"The ordinary Klansman is a dumb, illiterate, vicious clown," Garrity said. "But nothing but vicious applies to Mayfield. He waited two years until you built up a flourishing business before he decided it was time to take over. You're fighting Mayfield, not the Klan."

"Bringing in those rifles will be like a declaration of war," Kinnock said.

"That's what most countries do when they're attacked. They surrender or they fight back. Men and countries are the same. Mayfield declared war on you when his Klansmen started stealing cows and wrecking machinery. That was just skirmishing, but then he sent his men to bomb the meeting and to kill Durkin and anybody else who happened to be around. You were around."

Kinnock didn't answer and Garrity went on.

"Mayfield will be sure to hear about the rifles, and if by some chance he doesn't, then we have to make sure somebody tells him. Mayfield must know that you're getting set for him. Twenty-five thousand rounds is more ammunition than you'll ever need, so your fighting force—the men ready to fight for you and the ranch—can get plenty of target practice. I want the Kinnock ranch knee deep in shell casings."

Kinnock smiled his mournful smile. "How you exaggerate."

"Sure I do. But what I want you to do is whip up the men when you distribute the new rifles to a select group of men. Gone are the days when every man on a ranch knew how to use a rifle. Had to, to stay alive when Indians or raiders struck. The idea isn't to arm every man, just the best men you have. You were an army officer, you should know how to pick men. Tell the men the rifles are theirs for the keeping. Every man likes to get a new rifle. Don't fret about the cost. The colonel won't bill you and Maxim can afford it."

"I'm glad you're not my business manager, Garrity."

"I'd be no good at it. The men who work for you know they have good jobs and would like to keep them. You have about seventy men on the ranch. Select thirty, maybe forty, and tell them they're all that stands between disaster and Pig Meat Mayfield."

Kinnock actually laughed but it didn't last long. In an instant his long face was as gloomy as ever. "What a scoundrel you are, telling me to lie to my men. You know that's not true."

"If they think it's true it'll make them fight all the harder. What's important is for Mayfield to know that you're ready to fight and have the means to do it. It will make it that much easier if Mayfield has a spy on the ranch. Murdo says there can't be, but that's just his opinion."

"Murdo hires the men. He should know."

"How can he know? You've got hands from all over. Mayfield would want a spy on the ranch. Doesn't matter if there isn't. Some of your men go into town Saturday nights. They'll drink beer and boast."

Kinsella knocked and came in and told Kinnock he would have the conveyor belt working again in two to three hours.

"Good man, hard worker," Kinnock said after the Irishman went out. "That's what I like best—hard work. Garrity, tell me the truth. Do you think the rifles, all this training men and spreading rumors will make Mayfield decide it isn't worth it?"

"I doubt it. Mayfield wants what you have."

"Then what the hell do you think you're doing? Why bother?"

"Mayfield may not back off right away. I think it'll take some heavy fighting before he decides it isn't worth it. Sure he can get help from Klansmen in other counties, maybe even bring in hired gun-men, but it's a bit late in the day for that kind of thing. Worse, from Mayfield's point of view, it costs a lot of money. Men he brings in have to be housed and fed and armed and paid. I doubt if he'll go to that much trouble. Like I say, it's late in the day— this isn't 1850—and Mayfield can't get away with a dragged-out war. The president or the governor of Texas will have to step in if it drags on too long, gets too bloody."

"But it could go on for a long time."

"Pretty long. The Democrats will protect Mayfield

for a while, but even that can't last. Your best weapon is to make it too expensive for Mayfield to fight his war to the bitter end."

"Amen to that," Kinnock said.

Chapter Seven

It was Sunday and the plant was closed and the only men working at the ranch were those who had to. In the morning there was a prayer meeting conducted by Murdo, but few hands attended. For most of them Sunday was their day of rest. So why get up early to listen to a lot of preaching done by a bearlike man growling in a heavy Scottish accent? Kinnock didn't go to Murdo's service, but read the Bible in the main room of the house while Garrity cleaned the light Maxim on the other side of the fireplace.

Kinnock closed the Good Book and said, "You take such care of that murderous thing. No wife could be better cared for."

"If you're asking if I sleep with the light gun next to me, the answer is no. The gun is a good companion, but not in bed. For the real thing, I prefer a woman."

The Scots prude allowed himself a smile. "Speaking of women," he said. "How is it that you've never married?"

"How do you know I don't have a wife and ten kids back home?"

"You have no wife, no kids, no home. I just know. Please don't be offended."

"Why should I?" Garrity looked around the big comfortable room. "Why aren't you married? You have a fine house, a sound business, plenty of money. Don't tell me you're waiting till you find a woman with money."

"No, it isn't that. I'm waiting for the right woman. I don't want to make a mistake."

"What's wrong with making a mistake? Some of us learn by them."

"I don't want to learn by my mistakes," Kinnock said firmly. I'd rather wait and do it right. You're quite the opposite, I think. Tell me something if you don't mind. What's it like to live from day to day, with no responsibilities, no roots, no foundation to one's life?"

It was Garrity's turn to smile. "It's pretty good," he said. He didn't feel like telling Kinnock about the Zunis. "You get used to it after a while, and there's no turning back. Sometimes on a dark cold night in a strange town I pass a house and catch a glimpse of some family working hard at domestic bliss, Daddy reading, Mommy sewing, the kids playing, and I think that might not be so bad. The feeling always goes away when I'm in my hotel room with a no-strings woman beside me in bed, a stock of cold beer on top of the dresser. Even if I don't find a woman on short notice, there's always the beer."

"It doesn't sound like much of a life."

"Maybe not, but it suits me. There have been women who tried to lead me to the altar, and I was more or less ready to go. But in the long run I always heard alarm bells instead of wedding bells, and I ran for safety. There have been women who knew what I do and they said it would make no difference. They said they'd keep the home fires burning and welcome me back with open arms and open legs, no matter how long I stayed away. But I knew it wouldn't work. Women always try to change a man, no matter what they say. It's their nature. I've never met a woman from whore to Sunday school teacher who didn't want to keep her man on a string. My work doesn't allow for that. I don't want to worry about somebody and I don't want to be worried about."

Murdo came in slapping the dust from his clothes. Garrity wondered why he wore a thick tweed suit in the Texas summer heat. He knew Murdo had ridden out to spy on the guards he'd posted without telling Kinnock.

"A wee bit of a ruckus in the first bunkhouse," he told Kinnock. "Mahaffy and Lawlor got into a fight over something and I had to knock their heads together. Otherwise, it's a nice quiet Sunday afternoon. Not a sign of trouble."

Kinnock nodded. "Sit down and pour yourself a drink, Murdo. We were talking about marriage."

Murdo pretended to be alarmed. "I wouldn't go rushing into that. I been married five times, thrice without benefit of clergy. But I'm a God-fearing man and I never was married to more than one woman at the same time." Murdo made himself a drink and sat down. "In case you're wondering about the two I married legal, one died and the other claimed we weren't rightly married because the parson that married us had no right to preach. That's what she said,

98

and I believed her. Fact is I was glad to get rid of her. But there's nothing like a hefty warm woman on a cold winter's night. I might even get married again."

"Do we know the lady?" Kinnock asked.

"She's a widow woman in Amarillo," Murdo said. "Does fancy sewing and has a bit of money put by. A mite old for me though—she must be all of forty."

They heard the clatter of hoofs and then shouting when the rider reined in. A cowhand came in without knocking, a skinny kid of about twenty. He was excited, but tried to get hold of himself when he saw Murdo scowling at him.

"Pig Meat Mayfield's on his way in from the gate," he said to Murdo. "Says he wants to talk to Kinnock. Just himself in a buckboard, no bodyguards. Got some kind of a wild pig in a cage. I ask him why the pig and he says it's a gift for you, Kinnock."

Murdo snorted. "Two pigs in one buckboard." Murdo stood up and ground one hairy fist into the other. "Ye want me to turn him back, send him on his way?"

"Let him come in," Kinnock said. "Go out and meet him."

"Ye think that's wise? The man is a trickster and a buyer of murder. I told you he tried to bribe me."

Kinnock allowed himself a brief, sour smile. "And you called him a diseased sow. He can't have liked that, Murdo."

"Nor did I mean him to. To me he'll always be a pig with trousers on. At least a pig is a useful animal, while Mayfield is nothing but a feelthy scavenger."

Kinnock raised his hand to stop the Scotsman's tirade. "Do as I say. Go out and bring him in before one of the men gets a notion to shoot him."

"Not a bad idea at that," Murdo said before he went out.

"Has he ever been here before?" Garrity asked.

"Never has," Kinnock said. "We talked twice but on neutral ground, so to speak. Torrance's law office. I told him twice I didn't want to sell. Now I'll have to tell him a third time."

About five minutes later a buckboard rattled up close to the house. Murdo held the door open and Mayfield came in, grossly fat and not light on his feet the way some fat men are. His pinkish face was clean shaven, but with gray-white bristles on his triple chin. Murdo was right, Garrity decided. He did look like a pig in trousers. His gray lawyer-businessman's suit looked like it hadn't been cleaned since it was bought. There were grease stains on his vest and crotch. Everything about him was shabby, not the shabbiness of poverty because even the poorest man can keep himself clean. Even his wide-brimmed hat was shabby, with a thin hole worn through the crease and sweat stains above the band. People said he was a miser, Garrity thought, and he sure looked like one.

"Lord Kinnock," he said in a surprisingly clear voice, "it's been too long since we last talked and now I think it's time we talked again. Yes."

Kinnock stayed in his chair so he wouldn't have to shake Mayfield's hand. Instead, he waved him to a chair and offered him a drink.

Mayfield lowered himself into an armchair, filling it like an egg in an egg cup. "Thank you, sir," he said, smiling. "I'll drink anything as long as it's whiskey. No water."

Garrity was surprised that Mayfield didn't have a down-home accent. He probably did use one when he talked to the local folks, letting them know that he was as plain as an old shoe. His own shoes were plain enough, unblacked and with cracks in them.

Garrity poured the drink for Mayfield, not wanting Kinnock to wait on the greasy son of a bitch. Then he stood with his back against the rough stone of the fireplace.

"Your good health, sir." Mayfield raised his glass in salute and drank it off in two gulps.

"He brought you a wild pig," Murdo said angrily. "Bloody animal's the wildest thing I ever saw. Got tusks like razors on it. Creature like that could kill a man in no time. What d'ye want me to do with it?"

"Mr. Mayfield will be taking it back with him," Kinnock said.

"I urge you to try it, Lord Kinnock," Mayfield said. "No sweeter meat than the wild pig—they call it the javelina—from the Edwards Plateau. Wooded country down there and the javelinas run wild. No hog slop for those beauties: they live on nuts, berries, grass, bark, roots. They're carnivorous, of course, but their main food is nature's bounty. The result is lean meat instead of fat. Has a special flavor too." Mayfield smacked his lips. "I've got a whole pen full of them. Can't put them in with regular pigs, they're so fierce."

"What do you want, Mr. Mayfield?" Kinnock asked.

Mayfield drank the dribble of whiskey left in his glass. "To talk, sir. To spell out a few things so there will be no misunderstanding."

"Was there one?" Kinnock's question brought a growl from terrible-tempered Murdo. Garrity could well understand the Scotsman's impatience. All the polite British bullshit had no place there, not with a man like Mayfield.

"Sure there was." Mayfield set down his empty glass since nobody had made a move to refill it. "I made you a fair offer for the ranch and meat plant. You refused, so I'm about to make you a better offer. There won't be a third. I want to make that clear."

Murdo growled deep in his throat and Garrity knew that if Kinnock hadn't been there Mayfield would've been a dead or badly battered fat man. But Kinnock was there and Mayfield was counting on that to keep him safe. A look from Kinnock settled Murdo down and he sat there with a stone face.

"I won't sell to you at any price," Kinnock said. "You can offer double my investment and I'll still say no. I want to make that clear."

Mayfield wasn't at all put off by Kinnock's plain statement. "I wasn't going to offer you double, sir. What I'm prepared to offer you is half. I know you're an honest man and wouldn't think of cheating me. If we can go over your books together and agree on a figure, then I'm ready to pay you half that figure, no more, no less."

"Didn't I just tell you—"

"Hear me out, sir. Conditions here have changed since you made your investment, and what once was a quiet county is now seething with unrest. After lying dormant for nearly twenty years, the Ku Klux Klan has reformed and has returned to the terror of the Reconstruction Era. As you know, at first it was just threats and beatings. Houses have been burned. Your cattle and mine have been rustled. And now—I'm speaking of the other night, sir— it has come to killing." Mayfield looked at Garrity. "Your investment is in jeopardy. In short, you stand to lose everything."

Kinnock remained calm. "Thanks to you, Mayfield. Everybody knows you're behind the Klan."

"I ought to sue you for saying that," Mayfield said with a smile. "You have no proof of this terrible accusation and I dare you to repeat it in front of disinterested witnesses. However, I am not a litigious man and want nothing but peace. In fact, as a man of what might be considered old family in these parts, I have urged the Klan leaders to cease and desist for all our sakes."

"You say you talked to the Klan?"

"No. No. It wasn't like that. They won't talk to me face to face for fear that I would reveal their identities. I had to send written messages, not one but several. I'm afraid they refuse to listen. Worse than that, I am told. They say they are going to wash this county in blood. That's my latest information and it came to me the morning after seventeen of their number were killed, twelve in the street, five when the jail was stormed by masked men. You wouldn't know anything about that, would you, Lord Kinnock?"

Garrity had warned Kinnock to be ready for something like Mayfield's question. But he expected the accusation to come from the marshal, not Mayfield. "No, I wouldn't," Kinnock said. "Would you?"

"Me? Why would I have knowledge of such a dastardly deed? I've known most of those boys since childhood. What would I gain? You're talking nonsense, sir."

"What you'd gain is their silence," Kinnock said.

"Once again you're talking nonsense. I'm not accusing you of being behind the jailhouse lynching. But if you are guilty—just suppose you are guilty—what better way to throw off suspicion than to accuse someone else?"

Garrity wondered what would happen if he suddenly remembered that he was expecting an important telegram at the Lawton depot. All he had to do was ride out, wait for Mayfield and kill him from cover on his way back to his own ranch, which was south of town. To make it look good he could even ride on to the depot and ask about the telegram. Without a leader the Klan might fall apart. Then again, it might not. Mayfield's dummy congressman might come back from Washington and take it over. Or send someone in his place. The weak spot in his plan, a plan he liked very much, was that Kinnock would figure it out when he thought it over, and he'd order Garrity off the ranch and Garrity would have no base.

Mayfield was saying, "Ah well, those unfortunate boys are dead and there's no use dwelling on it. Perhaps we'll never know who killed them. But I must say this, Lord Kinnock: you are responsible for all the bloodshed in this once peaceful county."

"How is that, Mayfield?"

"You have disturbed the order of things, sir. Whites and blacks here lived in relative peace before you arrived with your highfalutin ideas, as our good country people call them. Twenty years ago, the Radical Republicans and the Freedman's Bureau sought to degrade the white man by establishing nigra supremacy. Five thousand Radical Republican teachers came south, not all to Texas, of course, to educate the blacks. Malicious mischief, no other word for it. Federal regiments, some of them black, backed them with bayonets and it was worth a white man's life to talk against them. It got so bad that no white woman was safe from insult or rape. And that, sir, is why the Klan was formed."

"I know all that," Kinnock said. "What's your point?"

But Mayfield was not to be rushed. "Why not let me have my say since this is the last time we'll talk? If you refuse to listen to reason, there is nothing I can do to help you. Even I will not be able to prevent the Klan from seeking a terrible revenge."

That's more like it, Garrity thought. Though he remained calm, Mayfield's voice had a little more edge to it.

"Talk as much as you like," Kinnock said. "Nothing you say will change my mind."

"So you say. But as I was saying, the original Klan lasted no more than five years, and it took martial law to stop them. Martial law in Texas! Think of it! Texas was an independent republic until 1845, at which time it was invited to join the United States and it graciously accepted. And then, less than thirty years later, it found itself ruled by the federal bayonet. But as time passed and the brutal Reconstruction faded, so did the Klan. The Klan disbanded because there was no longer any need of it. You look as if you're chomping at the bit, Mr. Garrity. Do you have a question?"

Garrity looked at Kinnock. It was his show, as Col. Pritchett would say. When Kinnock nodded, Garrity said, "Tell me this. If Kinnock canceled everything he's done—equal pay for blacks, closed their school—if he got rid of every black he's got working for him, would he still have trouble with the Klan?"

Mayfield smiled, then frowned. "I'm afraid so, Mr. Garrity. You see, once a thing gets started it's hard to stop it, in this case, impossible. Seventeen of their people are dead, and to them that's all that matters. Whatever else they may be, they firmly believe in the biblical eye for an eye. I'm afraid there can be no peace unless Lord Kinnock sells out and moves away."

"Sell out to you, you mean?"

"Not necessarily, sir." Mayfield's smile was as genial as before. "But don't you see I am the logical bidder since no one else in these parts has sufficient capital, or so my banker friends tell me. However, if someone has sufficient capital or could get it, I would have no hard feelings."

"You mean a dummy buyer? Maybe that ass-kisser you sent to Washington?"

Mayfield shrugged. "Nothing illegal in that."

Garrity said it straight: "What will happen if Kinnock doesn't sell?"

"Well, I can't really answer that, but I can guess at a few terrible things that might happen and probably will. Lord Kinnock's plant could be attacked in force, burned to the ground and all the men on the night shift killed. The railroad line to Amarillo could be dynamited. The same thing could happen to this fine house. Hoof-and-mouth disease could be spread among Lord Kinnock's herds. It can be spread by direct contact by diseased cattle or even the hides of cattle infected by the disease. There is no cure for it, as you probably know. The cattle just die or have to be destroyed. I've seen some fine herds wiped out that way."

"You'd go that far?" Kinnock asked in disbelief.

"I don't know why you keep on accusing me," Mayfield said. "It would have nothing to do with me. I swear it wouldn't. All I'm saying is what's possible. More than possible. You may think you can send for gunmen or private police, but the Klan can match you there. Match you and outnumber your hired gunmen. True believers will come to their aid, very hard men from the neighboring counties. I'm most reluctant to say this, Lord Kinnock, but there is no way you can keep from being killed if they decide to do it. The same goes for Mr. Garrity here, and not even his machine gun can protect him or yourself."

Murdo jumped up and would have thrown himself on Mayfield if Garrity and Kinnock hadn't wrestled him back into his chair. He kept on calling Mayfield a filthy pig Klansman until Kinnock pointed a stern finger at him.

"Let him finish," Kinnock said.

Mayfield took no heed of Murdo's outburst. "Mr. Garrity," he said, "I'm sure it will come as no surprise that the Klan has sworn to kill you no matter what. You and your machine gun did most of the killing, so my advice to you, and it's very good advice, is to take the next train out."

Mayfield heaved himself out of his chair. "I think that's all I have to say. Give my offer some thought, Lord Kinnock, and if you change your mind by the end of the week, please let me know. Good day to you, gentlemen."

Kinnock told Murdo to see Mayfield past the gate. The bitter old Scotsman muttered something, but followed Mayfield out. After they'd gone, Kinnock splashed whiskey into a glass and gulped it down, though as a rule he drank very little. As the whiskey took effect, his face twisted with the anger he'd been holding back. He reached for the bottle again, then corked it and shoved it aside.

"I'll have the law on that man," he said. "If it's the last thing I do I'm going to see Mayfield hanged or in jail. The law—"

"What law?" Garrity wanted to set Kinnock straight on West Texas law. "They got plenty of laws on the books here, same laws as the rest of Texas, but not much law. Getting Mayfield indicted, if you could manage to do it, wouldn't mean a thing. Some years back a newspaper photographer took a Kodak of a bigwig politician who was on trial for murder. This politician had a smuggled gun on him and got so mad he shot the photographer dead while he was snapping the picture. The prosecutor got the camera and developed the picture and it showed the politician firing the gun at the camera. Now you'd think that kind of evidence would convict him out of hand. It didn't. The jury acquitted him of the original murder. It acquitted him of murdering the photographer. Self-defense, the jury decided."

Kinnock made a helpless gesture with his large hands. "Then what can be done if the law here is like that?"

"The only way to get rid of Mayfield is to kill him. I'll kill him."

Kinnock turned his anger on Garrity. "You will do no such thing. I absolutely forbid it."

Garrity didn't like Kinnock's tone of voice. Where the hell did he think he was? He wasn't back in the Highlands where men settled their differences with their fists, unless the local constable stepped in and arrested them for disorderly conduct.

"I may kill him anyway," Garrity said.

"I think I better telegraph Col. Pritchett and have you ordered away from here. I'll not have murder talked of in my house."

"Seems to me you listened to plenty of murder talk just now. Your own murder was on the main bill. Mayfield meant every word he said."

"I know he did. But I cannot and will not countenance premeditated murder."

"That's the safest kind. You have time to do it right."

"I find your witticisms distasteful," Kinnock said, pursing his lips as if he'd bitten into a lemon. "The taking of human life is nothing to joke about."

Garrity was getting tired of all Kinnock's self-righteousness. Mayfield's intentions were clear: he had given Kinnock until the end of the week to change his mind. They had five days before Mayfield sent his Klansmen into an all-out war.

"Look," Garrity said. "You want me to stay or go?"

"I'd rather you stayed, but as I said before, it must be on my conditions. You must not kill Mayfield in cold blood."

Garrity decided his present predicament was the damnedest situation he'd ever been in. Kinnock was a man clearly marked for death if he didn't knuckle under and he wasn't doing anything about it. The dumb Scots bastard wasn't being asked to buckle on a gunbelt and meet Mayfield on Lawton's main street at high noon. Garrity wanted to laugh at the picture the idea brought to mind—Deacon Kinnock and Blubber Guts Mayfield—but of course he didn't. Why couldn't Kinnock be made to see sense?

"Let's do it this way," he said. "If I decide to kill Mayfield I'll tell you first and you can order me off the ranch. You can do it in town in front of what Mayfield calls disinterested witnesses. That way you'll be in the clear and I'll be free to work any way I want to. Is it a deal?"

Kinnock thought for a while. "For the moment it's a deal, but I don't like it. And I must tell you I'm not sure I won't feel it my moral duty to warn Mayfield."

Garrity hadn't expected Kinnock to go that far. Damn those Scotsmen and their Bible thumping!

"You won't warn him today? You won't chase him on a fast horse and spill the beans?"

Kinnock decided to have that second drink of whiskey. Garrity knew he was angry and didn't give a shit. "If I warn him—and I can't be sure I will— it won't be until you tell me. You're placing me in a terrible dilemma whether you know it or not."

"I don't mean to, Kinnock, and I don't sneer at what you believe in."

The second drink didn't go down as fast as the first one. Over the top of his glass, Kinnock said, "Have you no morals at all?"

"Mostly I'm on the side of the angels," Garrity said with a straight face. "I'd never shoot a poor widow with ten children to support unless there was no other way to keep her from killing me. And even then I'd try real hard to take the gun away from her. But I would kill Pig Meat Mayfield and feel good about it. I think it's every man's moral duty to kill Mayfield. Does that answer your question?"

"In a way, yes. What puzzles me is why you would want to do it on your own? Without help? Without men to back you up? You don't owe me anything and I'm fairly sure you don't like me. For my part, I like you well enough, but I don't approve of you. All those crates you brought with you when you came here, they're full of weapons, aren't they? Courtesy demands that I don't ask questions, but now I feel I must."

"They're full of weapons," Garrity said. "I was going to tell you, but so many things have happened. You want to look at them now?"

The two big drinks had calmed Kinnock and he settled back in his chair. He yawned and rubbed his eyelids. "I'm still tired, Garrity. Tomorrow will be time enough and you don't have to show me anything if you don't want to. You still haven't answered my question, you know. Why are you ready to risk your life for a man who won't cooperate with you? Is it pride in your work? Or is it because if you fail here it will be bad for your reputation?"

The answer to both questions was yes, but Garrity wasn't about to go into a song and dance about his pride and his reputation. Instead, he said, "I have to do it because I'll lose an awful lot of money if I don't."

"You mean you love money that much?" Kinnock's voice trailed off as he asked the question.

Garrity thought of the Zunis and how much he owed them. "When it comes to money, I'm Scotcher than you are."

He need not have answered. Kinnock was asleep.

Chapter Eight

Monday was much hotter than the day before. Murdo had gone to the plant before first light, taking ten men with him to be posted as guards until they got better organized. It didn't take much persuading to get Kinnock to agree to the move. Mayfield's threats had put deep lines in his face and he moved slowly, like a man trying to get his thoughts together.

Garrity and Kinnock were heading for the barn to uncrate the Motor Scout when Kinnock said, "What on earth is that?"

Garrity shaded his eyes against the sun and saw a tall ungainly figure limping up the road toward the ranch. They waited for the man to get closer and then Kinnock said, "It's that idiot boy from town. Is that a hatbox he's carrying?"

"Looks like it," Garrity said. "Stay where you are,

Kinnock. I said stay where you are. I'll see what it is."

Garrity walked out to meet the boy, but he didn't go all the way. The tall boy stopped when he did. "You're not Mr. Kinnock," he said slowly, dragging out his words. "I got something here for Mr. Kinnock."

"Put it down, son, and come ahead," Garrity ordered. "Do what I tell you, son. Mr. Kinnock is back there. Go talk to him. Come on now."

The idiot could have been any age between 15 and 30, and he had a long disjointed-looking body, dirty yellow hair, vacant blue eyes. He carried his head tilted to one side as he walked past Garrity without looking at him. Garrity drew his Colt and fired six bullets into the hatbox. Nothing happened.

"It's all right," he called back to Kinnock. "We'll look at it now. You talk to the kid. He doesn't know me."

Garrity walked to the bullet-riddled hatbox and opened it. In it was a black man's head and at first he didn't know whose head it had been. Then Kinnock came up close and said, "That's Lucky, the man you stopped the marshal from killing." Kinnock shuddered and looked as if he was going to vomit.

Garrity put the lid back on the box. In the heat the smell from the box was very bad. "Looks like they caught up with the poor bastard."

The idiot gave Garrity dirty looks because he had shot up the hatbox he had carried so far. But he told Kinnock that some man—just some man, he didn't know the man—gave him a dollar to carry the hatbox out to the ranch. Would he know the man if he saw him again, Kinnock wanted to know. He couldn't say, he didn't know—just some man.

Kinnock gave him a dollar, patted him on the

shoulder, and sent him on his way.

"This is monstrous," Kinnock said, gray faced with shock. "My God, who could do such a thing!"

"Lots of people," Garrity said. "Can I get you a drink? No drink, then where can I find a shovel?"

Garrity got a shovel from the barn and buried Lucky's head behind it. Some of the nighthawks, men who guarded the herd during the night, came out of the bunkhouse wanting to know what the shooting was about. Kinnock mumbled something and sent them back to their bunks.

"Now the question is," Garrity said, slapping the tiny grave flat, "what happened to the rest of him?"

Kinnock stared at him. "Is that all you have to say? Don't you have any feelings?"

"Feeling sorry for Lucky won't do any good. He should have kept his mouth shut. What Mayfield is saying is that what happened to Lucky can happen to you. You sure you don't want that drink?"

"I told you I didn't want it. If I look sick, it's because I am sick. The poor miserable drunken creature, to end up like this! I couldn't give him a job at the plant because he was drunk all the time. Every cent he could scrape together went for drink. Why did they have to kill him?"

Garrity was getting tired of Kinnock's lamentations. "Because he meant no more than a cockroach. He just happened to be handy. Sending his head would get your attention quicker than writing a letter or burning a cross in your front yard. Come on now, if you don't want a drink, let's go to work."

Kinnock sat on a barrel while Garrity used a hammer-ax to strip the sides of the crate away from the Motor Scout. Garrity checked it for damage, but there was none. The small armored vehicle gave off a dull gleam in the gray light of the barn. Kinnock

114

got up and walked around it.

"My Lord!" he said. "What an odd-looking contraption!"

"It takes some getting used to," Garrity said. "I've never used it, but the colonel says it works and I have to take his word for it." Garrity took a wrench from the tool kit and bolted the machine gun in place. "It runs on gasoline like any automobile. You fill the tank in back, crank the engine, and you're ready to go."

"Simply incredible!" Kinnock said.

Garrity was telling him about the speed of the Motor Scout when the barn door opened and a middle-aged black man came in. Both his hands were bandaged. He had grizzled gray hair and a cast in one eye.

"What is it, Lewis?" Kinnock asked.

The black man said, "Jus' came to tell you I kin work if you needs me. Pain ain't so bad now, boss."

"No need for that," Kinnock said. "We'll manage all right. Rest up and get well."

After he left, Garrity said, "He saw the Motor Scout?"

Kinnock didn't seem to think it was important. "What difference does it make? He's a good old man and has been with me for nearly two years."

"He isn't as old as he acts and two years isn't so long. What do you know about him?"

Kinnock frowned. "What are you going on about? Lewis is just a cook, and a damned good one at that." Kinnock went to the door, opened it, and looked out. "He doesn't have his ear to a crack if that's what you're thinking. I'm telling you, Lewis is just a cook."

"What do you know about him?" Garrity repeated.

"Oh, for God's sake, Garrity, keep this up and you'll have me suspecting Murdo. Lewis was a drover for the old trail herds before he turned to cooking. He's no French chef, but he cooks good plain food and that's what I like to eat. What do you find wrong with him?"

"He tried too hard not to look at the Motor Scout. Anyone else would have stared at it. There's nothing wrong with his eyes, is there?"

Kinnock shook his head. "Not that I ever noticed."

"Then let's go see if he's gone back to the bunkhouse. He sleeps in the bunkhouse with the rest of the black hands?"

"No, he sleeps in the shed where we keep the fence posts. Says he'd rather be by himself. If he wants to be uncomfortable, why should I care?"

"Let's look there. Hurry it up, Kinnock. If he's our spy, I don't want Mayfield to know about the Motor Scout. Get moving, man."

Garrity didn't push Kinnock out of the barn, but he came close to it. "This is madness," Kinnock kept saying. "You can't believe what you're saying."

They looked in the storage shed, but Lewis wasn't there. Kinnock kept yelling for him until one of the horse wranglers came to see what was wrong.

The man looked surprised. "Lewis cut out a horse and rode out a few minutes ago. Something wrong, Kinnock?"

"Did he have a gun?" Garrity asked. "A pistol? A rifle?"

"He had a rifle," the wrangler said. "I didn't know a cook could afford a rifle like that. Hey, Kinnock, it looked like one of your rifles. With the telescope sight. You think he stole it? Black bastard looked like he was heading for town."

Kinnock told the wrangler to go back to work.

"Padlock the barn," Garrity said. "I'm going after him. It won't be so good if he gets to Mayfield before I get to him. You say he used to be a drover?"

Kinnock nodded. "He still rides pretty good. You better take my horse, the big red Morgan. Listen to me. Don't just shoot Lewis down. We have no proof he did anything wrong."

"I'll find the proof," Garrity said.

The Morgan was a spirited, one-rider horse and it took Kinnock to calm him down. Garrity climbed into the saddle and Kinnock handed him a .44-40-caliber Winchester. "Easy on the bit," Kinnock said. "Let him have his head and he'll do his best for you."

Garrity took the big horse out onto the road at an easy canter, then touched his heels to the animal's side and felt the surge of power as the Morgan broke into an effortless gallop. The black cook had a fair lead, but Garrity knew the Morgan would overtake him within a few miles no matter how hard he rode. The catch was that the cook had a high-powered sporting rifle with a telescopic sight and all he had was a Winchester carbine. A fine weapon, but it didn't have the range. If the cook holed up in a good position, it would be hard to get at him. The man had to be killed—somehow he had to be killed—but only after he talked.

Garrity caught sight of him before he had gone four miles from the ranch. Past the gate of the ranch, Garrity saw him riding hard on the county road, flogging his mount right and left. The big Morgan began to close the distance between them. Low rocky hills were on both sides of the road, and after another half mile, with the Morgan closing fast, the cook took his horse off the road and rode up a long bare slope with a scatter of rocks at the top. Garrity saw him jump down holding the rifle; then the horse ran on and the cook took cover in the rocks.

Garrity was still in the saddle when the first bullet came at him. The high-powered bullet shattered the saddlehorn and whined on through. Garrity jumped down and whipped the Morgan away from there with his hat. The horse started to gallop back toward the ranch. Another bullet came close as Garrity dived into a clump of brush by the side of the road. He figured the cook could shoot better than that. All he was doing for the moment was trying to keep Garrity pinned down while he worked his way into a better position.

The slope was long and bare and the telescopic sight gave the cook all the advantage. With the sight he could see an insect on a leaf. A man's head would loom big in the crosshairs. Now and then the big sporting rifle boomed and a bullet tore into the brush. Garrity knew Mayfield's black spy had plenty of ammunition or he wouldn't be wasting it like that. If he had filled his pockets with shells, and no doubt he had, he could keep shooting all day.

Garrity didn't rise up to return fire because of the carbine's limited range. The firing stopped for a while and he wondered if the cook had gone down the far side of the slope. If he'd done that and found the horse, there was nothing to keep him from getting to Mayfield. Garrity raised his hat on a broken branch and a split second later a bullet blew it away. If he hadn't rolled fast a second bullet would have ripped through his chest. He lay still, protected by nothing but brush, but no more bullets came.

He couldn't rise up to look at the slope, but he remembered there were rocks scattered about halfway to the top. Not big rocks and not all together,

118

but some sort of cover. If no more bullets came, he had no way of knowing if the cook had gone down the far side of the slope or was just holding his fire, waiting for a better shot. Waiting him out until it got dark was no good because he could be miles away by then.

The brush grew along the bottom of the ridge and he crawled to the middle of it trying not to shake it up too much. After he got there he lay still for a good ten minutes before the big rifle boomed again and when it did he jumped and loosed off three shots, working the loading lever as fast as he could. The cook must have ducked instinctively and when he fired again Garrity was already running zigzag up the slope like an Apache, touching the ground with the tips of his fingers, using the slight leverage to spring from side to side. Bullets followed his run without hitting him. The sporting rifle was a bolt action and the cook knew how to use it. But he was still bolting shells when Garrity threw himself down behind a small pile of rocks.

He lay there while the cook shot at his position. The bullets were spaced far apart as if the man meant to wear him down with slow, steady fire. It was close to noon and hot as hell on the shaly slope. Then the shooting stopped and when he took a chance and jumped to his feet, bracing himself for a bullet in the chest, nothing happened. Then he ran to the top of the slope and over it and from where he was he saw the cook about 200 yards below, running as fast as he could, and at the same time he saw the horse not too far off standing in a patch of sun-yellowed grass. Garrity fired at the running man without much chance of hitting him, but the gunfire made the horse run away. The cook ran on, but he was a man in his fifties and after one last desperate spurt he ran slower and slower. Then he stopped and turned and tried to aim the big rifle. He got off a shot and it missed and he tried for another one and that missed too. He started to run again, but it was no good. He was just too old for running. Now he was coming into range and Garrity fired two shots at his legs and missed. Garrity ran on until he was close enough for a better shot. He stopped and aimed and fired shots at the cook's legs and brought him down with one of the bullets. The cook pitched forward and the rifle flew out of his hands, landing in thick brush. He was trying to get at it when Garrity came up behind him and told him he was a dead man if he didn't stay still.

"Turn over with your hands behind your head," Garrity said.

"I don't do nothing for you, white devil," the cook said. "Shoot me all you want. I don't turn, I don't put my hands on my head. You think I'm afraid of you? Do your worst, white satan. You already done your worst to me, what more can you do?"

Garrity held the Winchester steady on the back of the cook's head. One thing was for sure: the man wasn't afraid to die. Threatening to kill him wouldn't make him talk. Torture wouldn't work either. Garrity was sure of that. He had to try something else.

"I don't want to do anything to you," Garrity said. "All I want to know is why you spied for Mayfield. Mayfield is the boss Klansman here and he hates the black man like poison. Why would you want to work for a son of a bitch like that?"

The cook didn't turn his head. "Every white man hates the black man. Man like Kinnock pretend to like the black man. Mayfield don't try to hide his hate. I like that better. Least you know where you stand with a mean white man like he is."

"How much is he paying you? Ten dollars a month?"

"Mayfield pay me fifty." Suddenly the cook turned to face Garrity, but he didn't put his hands on his head. Garrity pointed the rifle at his face. "Go slow, Lewis."

The cook tried to spit at him, but it was hard to do lying on his back. "Don't you call me Lewis. I don't know you, devil."

Garrity didn't shift the carbine from the black man's face. "You can't bullshit me. Mayfield never paid you fifty dollars a month. You know why? Because a dirty man like you isn't worth it. Tell the truth. Mayfield paid you ten. Maybe he paid you five. Maybe you spied for a few bottles of rotgut whiskey."

"Mayfield pay me fifty," the cook said. "That's what he pay me. I don't care you believe me or not."

"Maybe I believe you," Garrity said. "It's pretty good money, but how would you like to make a lot more?"

Lewis showed broken teeth in a sly grin. "Doing what, you lying white devil?"

"Spying on Mayfield for Kinnock. He'll pay you two hundred a month to spy on Mayfield. We'll give you information to pass on to Mayfield so he'll think you're real smart, but all the time you'll be working for Kinnock."

The offer got another sly grin. The man was completely crazy, Garrity decided. Crazy and dangerous. It didn't matter what had made him crazy.

"You talk big, devil," the cook said, grinning like a mean dog trying to sneak close enough to bite, "but Mayfield count out the dollars and you don't show shit."

Holding the carbine in the crook of his arm, Garrity counted out $200 in tens and twenties, then reached down and stuffed the money in the black man's pocket. He took it out and counted it himself before he put it away.

"How'd you know I won't tell you lies 'bout Mayfield?"

"I'd find you and kill you if you did that."

"You ain't so tough, devil. I'm tough. You shoot me in the leg and I don't holler and howl."

"That's because I hit you in the heel of your boot."

Lewis laughed like the crazy man he was. "You ain't so dumb. I thought I had you foxed. All right, I don't lie to you 'bout Mayfield. You let me go there now, I come back tonight and tell you plenty. Mayfield think I'm a crazy and don't think I listen close to what he say, you twig?"

"I twig. But what can you tell me about him now?"

"Well, he talk a lot to that Whittaker, specially when the two of them gets drunk and sit up half the night. I been there at night two or three times. Easy for me to do that. I just sneak off the ranch and nobody see me. Last time I was there Whittaker keep saying how he got to kill you and Mayfield come right back at him and yell why don't he do it and stop bullshitting 'bout it. Then another night they was talking about how to spread hoof-and-mouth amongst Kinnock's herd and Whittaker tell Mayfield he can get a sick cow's hide from a vet over in the next county. You tell Kinnock to watch his cows, Garrity. You tell Kinnock Lewis give it to you straight."

"You ever hear them talking about a black man called Lucky? Lived in Lawton, did odd jobs."

Lewis laughed as if Garrity had made a joke. "That drunk. Mayfield feed him to the wild pigs after Whittaker cut off his head. Whittaker like to laugh 'bout it."

Jesus Christ! To kill a man like that and then laugh about it. "What else?" Garrity asked. "You don't have to lie there. Sit up or stand up."

Lewis got up but Garrity didn't moved the carbine far from him. "You ruin a good pair of boots, Garrity. Well, the only other thing I can tell you is one night, just the other night, the two of them was talking about old Murdo. It look like Mayfield have a real hate for him 'cause he call Mayfield a dirty pig and that kind of shit. Whittaker say to Mayfield, 'Why don't we kill the old Scots son of a bitch. Kinnock depend on him for everything. Without that old man, Kinnock don't know how to wipe his ass when he shit.' Mayfield like that and he say let's us think about doing that. Listen here, Garrity, don't ask me no more questions. Let me go to Mayfield and I bring back plenty of news."

"Sure," Garrity said. "Go catch your horse."

Lewis turned and Garrity shot him in the back of the head, then took the $200 from his pocket. Poor crazy bastard! He couldn't be trusted, so he had to be killed. Garrity took no pleasure in killing the black man. Killing Whittaker and Mayfield—especially Mayfield—would be altogether different. He looked forward to killing Mayfield in the cruelest way he could think of.

He caught the cook's horse and rode it back to the ranch. The Morgan horse had made its way back there hours before. Kinnock was waiting in front of the house when he reined in and climbed down. "I thought you must be dead when the Morgan came back without you. I took some men and rode most of the way to town, then turned back. Where were you, for God's sake?"

"On the other side of a hill listening to the cook. He admitted spying for Mayfield, said he got fifty dollars a month for doing it. I offered him two hundred a month to spy for us. He agreed to do it and told me a lot of things we'd never have found out by ourselves. One of them was that Whittaker cut off Lucky's head and Mayfield fed the body to his javelinas."

The blood drained from Kinnock's face and he clenched his fists. "It's like a nightmare."

"No nightmare. Lucky said they did it and I believe him. It figures, so I believe him. They're fixing to infect your herd with hoof-and-mouth, but you already know that. But listen to this. They're planning to kill Murdo. Mayfield hates him and wants to kill him for calling him a dirty pig. At the same time he wants to deprive you of your righthand man."

"He is that, old Murdo."

"Where is he?" Garrity asked. "I heard him going out at first light. You tell him to stay this long at the plant?"

"I gave him no specific orders," Kinnock said. "Murdo is pretty much his own boss unless I tell him otherwise. But it's late in the day and he should be back. What do you think we should do?"

The wrangler came to take Garrity's horse. "Wait a while. If he's not back by dark, we should go looking for him."

Kinnock tried to cheer up. "Murdo is a tough old bird and can take care of himself. Come and have a bottle of beer. I had some sent out from town."

"I'd like nothing better," Garrity said.

Kinnock hesitated. "What happened to Lewis the cook?"

"He tried to grab my gun and rob me at the very last minute. I had to kill him, nothing else I could do."

"I see," Kinnock said.

A little later, drinking whiskey while Garrity drank beer, Kinnock said, "The odd thing is Murdo never liked Lewis. Once I asked him why and he said he couldn't explain it."

Garrity took a healthy swallow of good Pearl beer. "Then Murdo didn't hire him? He told me he hired all the men."

"Not Lewis. I hired him myself. Murdo was right, after all. I should have listened to that old rascal."

"Look," Garrity said. "I wish you'd stop worrying about Murdo. I think Lewis was telling the truth, but Mayfield did give you till the end of the week. He'd hardly try to harm Murdo before then."

Kinnock drained his glass and refilled it. "I'm beginning to believe Mayfield is capable of any outrage. You've been telling me that since the first day you arrived here. I didn't want to listen because I'm a very stupid man. But you were right and Murdo has always been right about Mayfield—and I was wrong."

"All right, you've said it. You don't have to keep saying it. Settle down so I can enjoy my beer. It's not dark yet. When it is, we'll start looking for Murdo. Most likely he'll be good and mad at us."

Kinnock filled his glass again. "Good old Murdo, salt of the earth," he said, slurring his words a little.

Kinnock was drinking too much and Garrity didn't

125

like it. The trouble with men who drank very little was they drank too much when they got started. He didn't want Kinnock staggering drunk if the trouble with Mayfield suddenly boiled over. He had a bad feeling about Murdo, but refused to decide about it one way or another. He knew time would decide for him.

He was glad when Kinnock fell asleep in his chair, his head tilted back, snoring loudly. It got dark but Garrity let him sleep. Time enough to wake him in another hour or so, when the effects of the whiskey would have worn off. But just then Kinnock woke up looking frightened. It seemed to take him a while before he knew who Garrity was. Before Garrity could stop him, he slopped whiskey into a glass and gulped it down. He went to his desk and took out a canvas belt and holster with a British Webley .455-caliber revolver in it. While he was buckling it on, he said angrily, "Why didn't you wake me, Garrity? You shouldn't have let me sleep."

Garrity said nothing. One big drink and Kinnock was drunk again, and before they left he took another one. "What about the men?" Garrity asked as they headed for the corral.

Kinnock staggered slightly. "We don't need the men. We'll do this ourselves. If you don't want to help me look for Murdo, stay here and drink your beer."

Garrity wanted to tell Kinnock to go to hell, but he didn't. Kinnock was suddenly losing control after holding himself for too many years on too tight a rein. Garrity wanted to kick his ass, but he couldn't let him ride off into the darkness, drunk and confused. The Morgan horse far outdistanced Garrity's gelding, and he made no real effort to catch up. The only thing he could hope for was that Kinnock wouldn't take a fall and break his neck. When he did finally catch up, Kinnock was reined in and staring at Murdo's body hanging by the neck from the crosspiece of the gate.

The moon was bright enough to see by, and Kinnock continued to stare at Murdo's corpse long after Garrity said they should cut it down. Kinnock didn't answer and Garrity just sat his saddle, waiting. About five minutes passed and then Kinnock said, "We better take him home, Garrity."

"I'll do it," Garrity said, and while he was taking down the body, making sure it didn't drop to the ground, Murdo's horse came nosing along the side of the road. Murdo's hands were tied behind his back and it looked as if they had hanged him from his own horse. The horse nearly spooked when Garrity eased the body over the saddle and secured the hands and feet with a rope.

Kinnock rode ahead and Garrity followed slowly, leading Murdo's horse. It seemed to take a long time to get back to the ranch. Murdo had had a house of his own, but Kinnock insisted that the body be laid out in the main room of his house. Kinnock didn't give a reason and Garrity didn't ask for one.

Garrity put the body on the sofa because there was nowhere else to put it. Kinnock drank three quick drinks while he was doing that. The whole thing was dumb, Garrity thought. Murdo's body should have been put in his house until a coffin was made or one was brought out from town. Murdo's death didn't mean a lot to Garrity, who had seen too much sudden death to be easily moved by it. Besides, he hadn't known the man very well. Just the same, the Scotsman was a lusty old bastard who had enjoyed his windbagging tales and his hefty warm women. Mayfield would have to be made to pay for his death.

But first Kinnock had to be brought into line.

Chapter Nine

Garrity knew he'd have to do something when he turned away from the body and saw Kinnock trying to load the heavy British revolver. The Webley was a break top, meaning that when a catch was pushed the barrel and cylinder could be hinged down for loading and unloading. Kinnock was loading bullets and not doing a good job of it. At least ten cartridges rattled to the floor before the pistol was fully loaded and he snapped it shut.

He looked at Garrity with unfocused eyes, brandishing the Webley at the same time. "You know, this thing wasn't even loaded. In the bloody Scots Guards they'd have me up on charges if they found out."

Garrity didn't tell Kinnock to take it easy because sometimes telling drunks that got them mad.

Kinnock drank another big drink, then flopped back into his chair. "Where's Murdo?"

"Murdo's dead and lying on the couch," Garrity said.

Kinnock still had the gun in his hand. "Mayfield has to pay for killing Murdo," he shouted, waving the gun. Without warning he fired three shots into the roof of the house, bringing down dust and splinters of wood. "Murdo must be avenged! Turn out the men! We'll burn out Mayfield and hang him from the nearest tree!"

Kinnock was still shouting when Garrity got behind him and rabbit punched him in the back of the neck, catching him before he hit the floor. He hid the whiskey and the revolver behind some books before he carried Kinnock into bed.

Garrity got a bottle of beer from the kitchen and sat looking at Murdo's corpse. When he got tired of that, he covered the body with a blanket. He found himself smiling in spite of all that had happened. Kinnock, after all his pacifist bullshit, was finally rearing to go, but tonight wasn't the time. Mayfield wouldn't have ordered Murdo's kidnapping and murder if he wasn't ready for a fight. He'd be holed up in his big house, hiding behind a wall of Klan riflemen. And when the death of Murdo failed to provoke a disastrous attack, morning would find him trying to make new plans.

Before he went to his room, Garrity got another bottle of beer and looked in to see how Kinnock was doing. He lay on his back, snoring. It could get cold at night on the high plains, so Garrity covered him with a blanket. Garrity went to his room, drank the beer, and fell asleep in minutes. During the night he was awakened by Kinnock's mumbling, but that stopped after a while and he went back to sleep.

Kinnock was still asleep when he got up at first

light and made a big pot of strong coffee. Then he cooked breakfast, steak and eggs, and waited for Kinnock to come to life. He was in no hurry to see that. Drunk or sober, Kinnock could be a pain in the ass.

An hour later, Kinnock stumbled into the main room while Garrity was measuring Murdo for his coffin. Murdo wasn't tall, but he was very wide. Garrity wrote down the measurements and turned to Kinnock. "How do you feel?"

"Angry." Kinnock stared at the corpse. "Angrier than I've ever felt in my life. In a way I blame myself for Murdo's death. How many times did he say we had to put the fear of God in Mayfield before he got worse? What he really meant was before Mayfield destroyed us. But I wouldn't listen and there lies Murdo dead."

Garrity covered the body. It would have to be moved soon, before the day got hot. In the West Texas summer a body started to stink in hours.

"What could you have done?" Garrity asked.

"I could have walked up to Mayfield and shot him dead."

"Bullshit! They'd have hanged you. You have to settle down, Kinnock. We'll take the war to Mayfield, but we're not ready to do it right this minute. The shipment of rifles hasn't arrived. I have to check on that today. Without the rifles, without a plan, Mayfield could grind us into the dirt."

"Mayfield is just one man. All it takes is one bullet."

"That's true, but how do you get at him? I haven't scouted his house yet, but it has to be guarded like the Denver Mint. You can't get in there, Kinnock. Mayfield wants you to try—that's why he killed Murdo—but you're not going to do it."

Kinnock jumped to his feet. His hands were shaking. "Look who's talking caution. Where's my revolver, Garrity?"

Garrity was too pissed off to keep up the pointless argument. "Behind the books over there, third row. The whiskey is there too. I guess you could get a weapon and a bottle without much trouble. Drink up, you dumb son of a bitch. Last night you were going to lead the charge. Burn Mayfield out and hang him from the nearest tree. Why don't you try it now and see how many men will follow you in broad daylight. Or maybe you can kill him long range with the telescopic rifle I took back from the spying cook. Well, let me tell you something. You can lie up in the hills for a year and Mayfield won't show himself."

"I don't need you, Garrity." Kinnock took the revolver and the bottle from behind the books, but didn't leave the room. Instead, he put the gun and the bottle on a table and sat down next to it. He was still shaking, but Garrity couldn't decide if that was due to anger or the previous night's drunk.

"You don't know what you need," Garrity said. "You don't even know how you feel. One minute you're preaching brotherly love, the next you're crying bloody murder. Why don't you make up your mind which it is?"

Kinnock stared at the backs of his hands as if reading something there. "You can leave anytime you like," he said. "Tell the colonel I sent you packing and, while you're at it, tell the colonel to mind his own bloody business. That will be all, Garrity."

Garrity laughed, something he rarely did. "So you're the little lord of the manor after all? I always pegged that call-me-Kinnock stuff as a lot of bullshit. It's shit and you're full of it. One last thing I'm

going to tell you, which is I'll ride out right now if
that's what you want. But if you want me to stay,
it has to be on my terms. That's what you told me,
remember? You hear me, your lordship?"

"I hear you."

"Then hear me good. You're not going to get
Mayfield on your own and I think you know it.
When I say Mayfield I mean Billy Whittaker as well.
One orders the murders, the other carries them out
or has them done. The way I see it, they both have
to die or there's no justice. That's why you can't fuck
this up with your boys' book notions. So forget about
turning yourself into a human bomb and killing both
bastards at the same time. I'm telling you there's no
way you can get at Mayfield. It can't be done, at least
not in the ways you're thinking about."

"How do you know what I'm thinking?" Kinnock's
voice was sullen.

"Because I've met your kind of man before."

"What kind is that?"

"Pretty goddamn dumb, that's what. A few of
them learned to think straight. You're a smart man,
Kinnock. Use your brain."

Some of Kinnock's anger faded and he said, "How
do you plan to get at Mayfield? Kill Mayfield and
Whittaker?"

"I plan to plan," Garrity said. "We have to get the
rifles and you have to pick the best men to use
them. The plant is more vulnerable than the ranch,
but both have to be defended. The ranch boundaries
have to be patrolled before Mayfield starts his hoof-
and-mouth plague. Talk to the foremen at the plant
and get rid of every man they even suspect of being
unreliable. How are the foremen themselves?"

Kinnock said, "They're not local men. No local
men knew how to do the job. Kinsella is from

Chicago. Dettrick and Bannerman are from Omaha. They're good men, all three."

"Same thing goes for the men on the ranch. The local men, from Lawton or nearby counties, have to be watched. Maybe that's not fair, but you have to do it just the same. How about the foreman? Murdo had no good word for him."

Kinnock looked at Murdo's blanket-covered body. "Murdo thought he was after his job. He wasn't. He preferred range work to sitting in an office. He's a local man but you can trust him to the hilt. He's a cousin of the man Whittaker tried to castrate. They're cousins, but more like brothers. He'd love to get the chance to take the knife to Whittaker."

"He'll get it. What about the man Whittaker tried to cut?"

"He has a tiny spread some miles north of here. Very poor people."

"See if the foreman can get him to come in with us. Men like him could win us this war. And now you're going to have to listen to something you probably won't like."

Kinnock gave a wary look. "What is it?"

"I'm going to try to get Durkin's help. How do you feel about that?"

"Go on."

"Durkin is a very hard men and the twelve men with him, if not as hard, are hard enough. They've got guns and they know how to use them and have used them. Maybe they're thugs, but we need them more than bank examiners."

Kinnock pursed his lips, a habit Garrity found irritating. "How would Durkin profit by fighting on our side?"

"He can't organize a meat plant that isn't there. He can forget about organizing the ranch hands. I know them better than he does and they won't join his union. They'll shoot him if he pushes them too hard. The meat plant, on the other hand, is his only hope of success in Lawton County. I think he'd like to go back to the national headquarters with a lot of new union members on the rolls. What do you care if he claims you pay such high wages because he forced you to?"

Kinnock didn't take kindly to that. "Why can't I just offer him money? I'll pay anything within reason."

"That might rub him the wrong way. Durkin may look like a skid-row prizefighter with too many fights under his belt, too many bells in his head. But behind that ugly mug is a man of principle. I'm only guessing, but I think I'm right."

A full minute went by while Kinnock thought it over. "What would it take then?"

Garrity grinned. "You'd have to let him sign up—organize—the men in your plant. I know you don't want to do it, but think about this. You can always double-cross him later. Have the men tear up their cards and tell Durkin to go to hell or back to Seattle."

That brought Kinnock's stark Scots honesty to the fore. "I'd never do that. If I made a deal with him, good or bad, I'd keep it. You really think we need him?"

"You bet. Thirteen tough, well-armed union men would do a lot to keep the plant from being destroyed. I pity the Klansman they get in a dark corner. He'd don no more sheets, burn no more crosses. I think it's worth it, Kinnock."

"Then I'm agreeable if Durkin is. How do I talk to him? Does he come here? Do I go to town?"

"I'd like to sound him out first. You're a lord and he's a roughneck and you might not get along if I don't wax the dance floor. You stay here and get Murdo buried." Garrity handed Kinnock the piece of notepaper with Murdo's measurements on it.

Kinnock took the Webley revolver from the table. "It doesn't matter who buries Murdo. You want me to go with you?"

"Stay here and get Murdo buried," Garrity said again. "If there's trouble in town, I'll try to duck it. If there's not I'll see what's doing at the plant. Might not be a bad idea for Durkin to move in today. You could talk to him there. It's the kind of territory you both know."

"You missed your calling, Garrity." Kinnock's smile was sad but real. "You always know what to do, what to say. I never do. You should have been a confidence man."

"Too risky. Pull yourself together, Kinnock, and no heavy drinking. You know the old saying. Lips that touch liquor shall never touch mine."

Though Murdo lay cold on the couch, Kinnock attempted a joke. "I don't have to kiss Durkin, do I?"

"Only if you have to and then put your heart into it. We need that ugly Irishman. I'll be back later and tell you what he says."

Holding the door open for Garrity, Kinnock said, "What if he says no to everything?"

"Then we'll run him out of Lawton County after we get rid of Mayfield and Whittaker. I'm not joking, Kinnock. I mean to do it. He's in or he's out all the way. I think he'll get the idea after it's explained to him."

Two of Durkin's shotgun men were sitting on the porch of the hotel when Garrity rode up. They regarded him with the dull flat stares of men who trust no one. Main Street was deserted, its sunbaked buildings silent in the sun, and even the saloon was quiet. It was baking hot and the wind was full of reddish dust.

"Where's Durkin?" Garrity asked.

"Not here," one of the men said. "Tell me what you want and I'll tell him when he comes back."

"Tell him yourself," the other man said to Garrity. "Here he comes now."

Durkin came up the street like a man who owned the town, a forbidding figure, with his black suit and hat, his savage, arrogant face. Garrity got down from his horse before Durkin got close.

"I'd like to talk to you," he said.

"Why not," Durkin said. He came up onto the porch and the two men went inside.

They sat in the rockers the guards had been in. Durkin took off his hat and threw it on another chair. His stiff black hair was laced with gray hair clipped short in a Prussian cut. It did nothing to improve his appearance. Nothing would, Garrity thought.

"I'm going to have a beer," Durkin said. "You want a beer?"

Durkin whistled for two beers and handed a bottle to Garrity. "No ice in this burg," he said. "I hear they murdered the old Scotsman. Hung him from the gatepost."

Garrity didn't ask how he knew. "They'll keep on killing unless somebody stops them."

"Nobody has yet." Durkin drank some of his beer. "They killed the lawyer sometime last night. Cut his throat."

"Torrance!" Garrity was jolted in spite of himself.

"The hardware man who owns the building, has the store downstairs, found him early this morning. Blood was leaking through the ceiling. An awful lot of blood. Looks like they started to cut off his head, but gave up on it or something scared them off. The lawyer's head was hanging by strings."

Whittaker! Garrity thought. Whittaker had cut off the drunken black man's head and sent it to Kinnock in a hatbox. The hatbox would have been Mayfield's idea. Whittaker didn't have enough imagination to think up the hatbox.

"That would be Billy Whittaker's doing," Garrity said. He told Durkin about the head in the hatbox, the killing of the spying cook.

"They're busy little bees." Durkin set down his empty bottle. "What did you want to talk about?" He whistled for two more beers.

Garrity laid the plan out, kept it short, and when he finished Durkin said, "We don't have to make a deal with Kinnock to unionize his plant. We can do it with or without a deal."

"Won't be much to unionize if all that's left is blackened boards and twisted machinery."

Durkin gave Garrity a bitter smile. "Kinnock is a rich man. He'll build a new meat factory and we'll unionize that."

"If there's a new plant, Kinnock will be gone or dead, and the new meat packer will be Pig Meat Mayfield. You won't unionize him."

Durkin did a little rocking. "You think we couldn't?"

"Not with twelve men, not with a hundred. You could send for every skullbuster in the Northwest and Mayfield would fight you to the bitter end. Quit the kidding, Durkin, I'm offering you a good deal, so stop wasting your time and mine. Come in with us

138

and you'll be protecting your investment."

"Investment!" Durkin made a spitting sound, but didn't spit. "You're starting to talk like a banker, Garrity. You've been hanging around rich men too long."

"Sure. You bet. Next I'll be wearing a silk hat."

"You'd look stupid in a silk hat. Tell me one thing though. What happens if I help save Kinnock's plant and then he decides what do I need this Durkin for? What if he says, 'Fuck Durkin and his union?' "

"I'd have to go after him if he did that."

"What would you do? Sue him for breach of promise?"

"I might burn his plant," Garrity said.

"I know I would," Durkin said. "And I'd burn him along with it."

"I can't fault you there. I'm talking for Kinnock. You can talk to him later. If you say yes, then the deal is made. So the deal is, in one way, between you and me. Kinnock's not the kind to pull a double cross, but should it happen, he'd have me for an enemy."

Durkin nodded, but made no comment.

"You can move into the plant today," Garrity said. "The sooner, the better. It will give Mayfield something to think about."

"Ain't that something now! Me with my own meat factory! Wait till the gees in Seattle hear about this!" Durkin laughed. He had false teeth, uppers and lowers. Col. Pritchett had a mouthful of false choppers, but his were the best money could buy. They were so real looking that some of them were slightly crooked and slightly stained by tobacco. Durkin's were obviously cut-rate and didn't fit too well. If Durkin was a thief, he didn't spend the money he stole on his teeth.

"Don't let your balls catch fire," Durkin said. "I'm not about to take over the meat factory, but you know I could run a meat factory. I worked in one in Omaha, more than a year. What a job for any human being! The blood, the guts, the stink! To this day I can't eat meat unless it's disguised every which way, like in meat loaf, goulash, junk like that. But I couldn't eat a rare steak if you put a gun to my head."

Garrity decided Durkin was a most peculiar man, a skullbuster who read books and had a weak stomach. It took all kinds.

"Mostly I eat fish," Durkin went on. "In Seattle I eat fish. Here I eat chicken. I guess you're not too interested in my health?"

"Sure I am. I want you healthy and strong if Billy Whittaker comes in the night with a can of kerosene."

"He'll wish he hadn't if I catch him."

"What about weapons?" Garrity said. "You have enough rifles and ammunition?"

"Mister, we have enough rifles and shotguns to start a war. Only one thing. You wouldn't like to sell me that machine gun? I always wanted to own one since I saw the one in England."

"Can't do it, Durkin. I can get you one just like it. Could be here in a week. A gift from me to you."

"I don't like gifts," Durkin said. "I pay or I take. What if I said no deal unless you sell me the gun?"

Garrity stood up. Maybe it was time they settled things. Durkin would keep pushing him till they did.

"You want more than the gun," he said. "If I sold you the gun, it wouldn't stop there. If I thought it would, I'd sell you the gun for a dollar. Forget the deal, we'll do it ourselves."

Durkin didn't say anything until Garrity was about to mount up. Then he said, "Whoa there! Let's us talk some more."

"What about the gun?" Garrity stood with the reins in his hand.

The rocker squeaked as Durkin set it in motion. "Well, sir, I'd like to have that gun, 'specially the way you have it tricked out, but I can see it has sentimental value. I was like that with my first pair of brass knuckles. Get me the gun you promised, all fitted out like yours, and it's a deal. What say we shake on it and have another beer."

Flies buzzed in the heat and an old man drove past in a wagon. The old man nodded and Durkin raised his bottle to acknowledge him. "Now there's a man too old to care about anything. Would be nice to be like that, at peace with the world. Of course he may be worrying some day they'll find his runaway young wife's body buried in the root cellar. They've got the lawyer's body in a coffin in the lumberyard. I went to take a look at it."

"Why is that?"

"Nobody else went to look at him, so I did. I wanted Mayfield to hear about it."

After a gulp of beer, Garrity said, "I have a big shipment of Winchesters coming in. Soon as they get here and we pick the right men we're going to hit Mayfield's ranch. That's the center of this whole thing. If Mayfield hasn't sloped off to general his war from afar, that's where he'll be."

"You'll have to kill a lot of rednecks to get at him. Dumb, ignorant bastards, but the ones who fight, fight like tigers. What beats me is why he has such influence with them."

"Because he tells them they're the noblest white men on God's green earth. Plays on their hate for blacks. Appeals to their patriotism. Lawton County is the only country they know."

A mangy dog came up onto the porch and looked expectantly at Durkin. "This dog likes beer better than biscuits," Durkin said. He poured a puddle of beer on the porch and the dog lapped it up, then lay down on its side. "Nice to have at least one friend in this dismal place. Garrity, what say we pool our forces and hit Mayfield together? Some of your cowboys may not fight too hard for a rich Scotsman."

"Some of them will, the ones who know what to expect if Mayfield takes over. Let's keep to the deal. You guard the plant and I'll go after Mayfield. You want to get your men together and go over there?"

Getting up, Durkin said, "They'll probably burn this place tonight. Had to buy it through a lawyer in Amarillo. Knew they wouldn't rent or sell to me. Fucking lawyer gouged me on the price."

"They can't burn the hotel without burning the town."

"Would be no great loss except for the beer," Durkin said.

They went to the plant, Garrity leading his horse, the dog staying close to Durkin, one of the union men driving a wagon with shotguns and rifles, ammunition boxes and battered grips in the back of it. If the marshal saw them, he didn't come out to look at them, but Garrity knew somebody on a fast horse would be on his way to Mayfield's place within minutes. There seemed to be no Klansmen in town and he figured they were lying low because killing a man like Torrance, a well-known lawyer and the son of a famous father, was a lot bigger than killing some black dirt farmer. Lawton was a frightened town waiting for all hell to break loose.

The man in charge of the guards from the ranch gave Garrity no argument when he said the union men would be taking over. "Durkin will give you your orders," Garrity said. "I have Kinnock's authority on that. Listen to Durkin. He's seen more fighting than any of us." Garrity added the last part so the man wouldn't feel left out.

Durkin took over Kinnock's bare office and sat behind the desk on the hard chair with his coat off. A ten-gauge shotgun and a Winchester rifle lay on the desk with a box of ammunition for both weapons.

"This is no office for a boss," he told Garrity, who was getting ready to leave. "If I'm here long enough I'm thinking of a carpet and a chair that won't break a man's ass. That can wait. What I am going to do is have the boys rig up some carbide lamps where they'll do the most good. The Klan doesn't like bright lights, but that's what they're going to get. We have some dynamite to make them feel at home. In our work we always need dynamite."

"I better get back."

"Tell Kinnock he can stop worrying about wrecked machines. Soon as you leave I'm going to take a tour and talk to the people. It's the mechanical meat saw for any machine breaker I catch with his little hammer or his pockets full of nuts and bolts."

"Go easy with the meat saws."

"That's just what I'll threaten them with. I won't cripple them so bad they won't be able to crawl away. The way I'll have things fixed up here, Pig Meat will have to puzzle his pig brain if he means to take this place."

Garrity didn't share Durkin's easy confidence. Mayfield hadn't become a political boss and a very rich man by making wrong moves. "If you run into heavy fighting—something so big you can't handle it—set fires in some empty barrels. Oily rags, waste, grease, anything that'll send up a lot of smoke. I'll post a rider close to town and he'll bring help."

Durkin just nodded.

Garrity rode back through town, still as dead as it had been, and there was a coded telegram from the colonel waiting for him at the depot. The shipment of rifles would be arriving in Amarillo at four o'clock on the following afternoon. There was no way the sleepy-eyed telegrapher could miss the way he cursed, crumpled the telegram form and stuffed it in his pocket.

"Something wrong?" the man asked, looking up from his newspaper. "I received it 'xactly the way it was sent. It being in gobbledygook, I had the other end sent it twice."

Garrity left without answering. A few minutes later, watching from the side of an old barn, he saw the kid who swept up around the depot saddle a horse and ride south through town.

Mayfield's ranch was south of town.

Chapter Ten

"We've got to move fast," Garrity said when he got back to the ranch. "Guns are coming in a special car that'll be added to the afternoon train to the plant. Wagons have to be waiting by the trackwalkers' hut by the bridge when the train comes. I saw the hut on the way here. About halfway between Aramillo and Lawton?"

Kinnock nodded. "About that."

"The spur-line conductor won't know about the special car till he's ready to leave. I doubt if he's taking money from Mayfield, but you never know. By now Mayfield knows I got a telegram, but that's all. I put on a show like I was mad about something, like maybe things weren't going right. I don't know. It could help. How far is the bridge from here?"

"I would think about forty miles. You'll have to take the wagons over back roads and old trails to avoid the road from Lawton."

"Who can get us there the fastest way?"

"Old Skeats can. He's a local man. You'll find it slow going in places. Nobody keeps up the old roads."

They were talking outside the house. It would be dark in a few hours. Garrity had told Kinnock about Durkin, but not about the lawyer's murder. But the time had come to tell him.

Kinnock took it calmly except for a sudden tightening of his thin mouth. "You didn't have to keep that for last. After Murdo I've been prepared for anything. We weren't really friends, but I thought Torrance a decent little man. Poor chap, he thought he was above it all . . . like I did."

Garrity went into the house to get the light gun and four grenades while Kinnock found Skeats and had the two wagons hitched up. By the time he checked the gun and drank a bottle of beer they were waiting for him. Two men were coming along to help load the guns. If all went well, they'd be back some time after midnight on the following night.

The back roads were bad, rutted and broken, and the old trails that linked them were worse. During the early hours of darkness they saw the lights of a few houses spaced miles apart. After that, nothing. Once a dog barked where there was no house, and there was no explanation for that. The dog stopped barking, but it followed the wagons for most of a mile, then dropped back into darkness. The weather turned colder and the men huddled in their lined coats as the wagons jolted over rocks or plowed through deep sand.

There was no moon, but Skeats, in the lead wagon, knew where he was going. They drank cold coffee from their canteens, and the only time they stopped was when somebody had to piss. Skeats drove one wagon, Garrity the other, and when it got late, the two ranch hands stretched out and slept. Skeats said they'd make better time going back because they'd be traveling by daylight. They saw the bridge and the railroad tracks about an hour after the sun came up.

They drove the wagons down under the bridge—the river was low in summer—unhitched the horses and let them drink. Skeats slept in the shade of the bridge while the two ranch hands went up on top to watch for trouble. The trackwalkers' hut was empty and the stove in it was cold. There were some hours to wait, but Garrity thought that was better than arriving with no time to spare and maybe walking into an ambush. That wasn't likely to happen, but Mayfield was a wily man with many sources of information.

On both sides of the track the country was flat and brown and featureless. Garrity climbed up high on the bridge and used his binoculars, but saw nothing. He did it again about an hour before the train was due to arrive; then he climbed down and told the men to hitch up the wagons.

"Looks like we're in the clear," he said.

He was looking at his watch when the train hooted in the distance. The horses stamped their hooves when they heard it. The train slowed and halted and the conductor swung down, nodded to Garrity, then walked back to the special car and undid the padlock. They got the wagons close to the open door and started to off-load the boxes of guns. The conductor said there were no passengers.

The train was across the bridge and gathering speed when Garrity spotted a dust cloud far down the track. He jerked the binoculars to his eyes and swore. Still far off but coming fast was a bunch of horsemen, some lost in the dust kicked up by the riders out in front.

"Take the wagons under the bridge and wait," he told Skeats, who was old but not as jittery as the two younger men. "I want them to look for us here."

The wagons rattled down under the bridge and Garrity waited, lying behind some sun-withered brush at the end of the bridge. The small amount of dust made by the wagons had settled, and it was quiet. On the bridge there were planked spaces on both sides of the track. That's where he would take them, when they were halfway across the bridge. He had the four grenades armed and ready by the time they got close.

They reined in before they got to the bridge, and there was a lot of shouting before they started across, the horses' hooves making hollow sounds on the thick wooden planks. Garrity stiffened when he saw the rider out in front was Billy Whittaker. The sun glinted on the long, shiny gun in his hand. It was too bad that Whittaker was going to die such a quick death.

Whittaker was turning to say something when Garrity opened fire, raking the bunched-up riders with bursts from the light gun. Men and horses screamed as bullets tore into them. All the lead riders were down, dead or dying, and the ones in back, not hit yet, were trying to get back off the bridge. Some of them were close to making it when he put the light gun down and threw the grenades, one after the other, over their heads. The grenades exploded seconds apart. Smoke boiled up and he picked up the light gun and fired into it, moving across the bridge, swinging the gun right and left. He stopped only when the last bullets rattled through the gun and there was nothing more to shoot at.

Nothing was left alive, not a man, not an animal. He went back to where Whittaker lay riddled with bullets and took the big Bowie knife from his belt. He wasn't sure why he took it. Maybe he'd use it on Mayfield. He gathered up all the other weapons he could find and took them down to the wagons.

They drove away leaving 18 dead men on the bridge. Getting back was easy. Garrity slept most of the way.

"I don't know how Mayfield found out, but he did," Garrity told Kinnock. "We can't waste any more time. We have to hit him now before he pulls any more tricks. Christ knows what he's planning. Maybe we're not ready, but we have to go after him. The bastard could be bringing in an army. Any word from town?"

"No smoke," Kinnock said. "Not a sign of smoke. How soon do you—"

"As soon as you get the men together. If Mayfield thinks Whittaker has the guns it may buy us some time. I'm saying that, but I just don't know. Mayfield may ease up, then again he may not. There's no telling what he'll do. Can we get close to his place without going through town?"

Old Skeats was standing by and he answered for Kinnock. "We can get there same way we got to the train. But Pig Meat could have men watching. Probably does. Do I got time for something to eat? But, you know, no matter how hard we travel, they's no way we can get even close afore full daylight. Middle of the day is more like it."

It was one o'clock in the morning and there wasn't much of a moon. Kinnock sent for the foreman and told him to get the men ready. The foreman's name was Hodges and he said the thin, silent man with

149

him was Andy Hodges. "Andy is my cousin, the man Whittaker—"

"Whittaker is dead," Garrity said to the foreman's cousin. "Too bad you couldn't have done it, Mr. Hodges."

The thin man shrugged. "Just as long as he's dead. I'd still like to go with you. Whittaker would have been nothing without Mayfield."

Garrity went to the barn to check the Motor Scout while Kinnock and Hodges were passing out the new Winchesters to 40 men. The rest of the men were to defend the ranch. Hodges had picked his best men, and those left behind would have to do their best if Mayfield's Klansmen came. Garrity wondered if they would, but it was now or never. Time was running out.

Garrity got into the Motor Scout and checked the machine gun and the two linked 300-round ammunition belts; then he put four more belts on the floor beside the driver's seat. He filled the tank with gasoline and fitted two additional cans of gasoline into the rack inside the vehicle. He cranked the engine to life, got back into the Scout, closed the door, and drove it out of the barn.

The vehicle had carbide lamps protected by bulletproof glass, but he didn't use them. No light of any kind could be shown no matter how dark it got. The motor, which sounded very loud inside the barn, didn't sound so loud when he got the Scout outside. None of the men had seen it before and they gaped at it in astonishment. The noise and the gasoline smell made the horses edgy, but they settled down before it was time to move out.

Skeats and Kinnock led the men while Garrity followed in the Motor Scout. The horses would be less likely to spook if they didn't have gasoline fumes blowing back at them. At first, they followed a trail that went miles to the south end of the enormous ranch. There the trail became an old road that wasn't used any more. The Motor Scout had shallow springs, but they were no match for the broken road, and Garrity hoped the goddamned thing wouldn't fall to pieces before the night was over. Behind him, the extra cans of gasoline sloshed steadily, a grim reminder of what could happen if just one bullet penetrated the light armor.

The hours dragged by and it got to be light and they took another road, with many miles still to go before they got close to Mayfield's place. They were five miles west of Lawton and Skeats said Mayfield's home ranch was another ten miles to the south. Skeats had worked for Mayfield years before, and he said they would be on Mayfield land after they passed a rock with an M painted on it in white.

They came to the painted rock and they stopped and Garrity got out to stretch his legs. The only air in the Scout Car came from the gun port and that was full of horse smell. It was good to stand up straight and breathe in clean air. The men sat their mounts while Garrity and Kinnock talked to Skeats.

Skeats described Mayfield's house as he remembered it—a long, low adobe house built in the Spanish style of early Texas. Many years after the original owner fled to Mexico during the Mexican War, the American adventurer who seized it had been forced out and Mayfield took possession.

"If he's there, there's no way to take him by surprise," Skeats said. "House is on a low hill in the middle of a grassy plain. Has got windbreak trees, but that's no kind of cover. They'll have us spotted before we get a couple of miles from the house. I'm here 'cause I'm paid to be here, but how are you going to do it, Kinnock?"

"I'll go in first in the Scout," Garrity said. "On the road I can move a lot faster than now. Soon as I get close enough they're going to cut loose with everything they have. If the Scout holds up the way it's supposed to, I should be able to run right up to the house with—"

"That tin can," Skeats cut in, shaking his head. "You say it'll stand up to bullets, but suppose one of the wheels falls off or you can't stop and run into the creek and can't get out? Then what do we do?"

"I don't know," Garrity said. "The wheels are bolted on tight and I'll watch out for the creek. One thing at a time. If I can keep them busy, the rest of you should be able to come in from two sides. You're the officer, Kinnock. How does it sound to you?"

"I can't think of anything else," Kinnock said. "You'll be the one bearing the brunt of it. You'll have surprise in your favor, if that means much. The grenades should help."

Garrity had given five grenades to Kinnock and kept five for himself. He had explained the grenades to Kinnock. After the safety plug was pulled out and the detonator screwed in, they were ready to throw. His own grenades, stuck inside his belt, were already armed.

"Let's go see Pig Meat," he said.

After another hour, they could see the house far out on the plain. It stood like a fortress on a slight elevation behind the windbreak trees. From the last patch of high ground he could find, Garrity scouted it with binoculars. On one side of the house and below it was a small lake made by damning the creek. Closer to the house, on the other side, were a barn, stables, a horse corral. Far out on the plain were vast numbers of cattle grazing in the sun. Garrity moved the binoculars back to the house and saw the pig pens. The binoculars brought them up close. One pen had ordinary pigs in it; the other had the javelinas, the ferocious wild pigs Mayfield liked to eat.

Looking at the javelinas, Garrity had an idea. But it could wait.

Kinnock and the others followed the Motor Scout at a steady trot until they reached the road that went on to the house. It was a good level road and Garrity increased his speed, leaving Kinnock and his men behind. A few minutes later he heard guns being fired and knew they'd been spotted. He pressed down the speed pedal on the floor and the Motor Scout surged forward without effort. He pressed down harder on the pedal until the Motor Scout reached its top speed of 25 miles an hour.

It went up the slight hill and through the gap in the trees; by then the Klansmen at the windows or in the courtyard were firing rifles at him. A hail of bullets hit the vehicle when the Klansmen got over their surprise and started to shoot straight. The Scout went up the hill with bullets whanging off its light armor. At the top, the road flattened out and he drove right into the courtyard and the men shooting at him from behind an old fountain scattered and made a break for the house.

Steering with one hand, firing the machine gun with the other, Garrity cut them down before they got to the door. He steered the Scout around the fountain, bumping over dead bodies, and drove along the side of the house, firing at the windows. Wood and glass and adobe shattered as a steady stream of bullets drove the defenders back from their positions. He turned and went back the way he had come.

Heavy fire came from the roof of the house and Garrity's ears rang as more and more lead was thrown at the Motor Scout. The house was in two sections and he drove along the side he hadn't hit yet. A bullet starred one side of the bulletproof window above the gun port. Another came through the port itself and hit the back of the vehicle behind his head. The road went around the house and he turned the Scout that way.

Four men were running down the back of the hill and he knocked them down with a burst. He went clear around the house, firing at the windows and doors. He couldn't elevate the gun enough to shoot at the men on the roof, and fire from there remained heavy.

The Motor Scout was back in front of the house when he saw Kinnock's men running up through the trees. He slowed the Motor Scout and raked the house with bullets to give them cover. A grenade exploded when he got past the big double doors. Two more grenades exploded and when he turned the Motor Scout again he saw Kinnock throwing his last grenade up onto the roof. The grenade was still falling when Kinnock was hit and went down.

Garrity drove the Motor Scout between him and the house and unlatched the door. Kinnock was hit in the side, but was trying to get up. Garrity grabbed the light gun and scrambled out of the Scout and dragged Kinnock into it and left him lying there with the door open. He threw two grenades through the door of the house and the house started to burn. But the bastards in there were still putting up a fight.

154

He looked behind him and saw that some of Kinnock's men were down, killed or wounded. The others were firing from the cover of the trees. He steadied the light gun on the roof of the Motor Scout and opened fire. He was still firing when a white cloth tied to a rifle barrel waved from one of the windows. He eased his finger back on the trigger and the surrender flag waved harder. Kinnock's men stopped firing, and it was quiet except for the crackling noise of the flames.

"We're coming out, we give up, don't shoot," somebody shouted. Other voices joined in, all yelling the same thing.

Garrity held the light gun steady on the door and yelled, "Come out one at a time, hands behind your heads. Come out quick!"

Kinnock's men moved in as the Klansmen came out, some staggering, some wounded, all blinded by smoke. Eleven Klansmen came out and Kinnock's men made them lie facedown and covered them with rifles. Hodges, the foreman, hadn't been hit and Garrity told him to look after Kinnock. Then Hodges tugged at his arm and he looked the way the foreman was nodding and saw Pig Meat Mayfield coming through the door, fat and wheezing and hardly able to walk. The steps were low and wide, but he staggered and fell and rolled before he got to the bottom. Garrity raised the light gun to riddle him with bullets, then changed his mind.

The javelinas! he thought. But that could wait. Garrity let him lie. He walked over to one of the Klansmen and kicked him hard in the side. "How many of you were there?"

"Near on thirty," the man said, his voice turning to a whine. "Please, mister, you don't want to kill us. We was just doing what Pig Meat said."

155

They had killed 19 Klansmen, but the figure wasn't right. Mayfield had a lot more men than that. He gave the Klansman another savage kick. "Where's the rest of you? Answer quick or I'll kill you sure."

"Pig Meat sent them to town," the man gasped, his face twisted with pain. "The meat plant! Sent them to burn the meat plant. Close on fifty men. I swear that's the truth. You don't want to kill us, mister."

Garrity kicked him in the side of the head to shut him up. He looked at Mayfield, but the fat man hadn't moved. The javelinas! Garrity thought again. Hodges had Kinnock out of the Motor Scout and was looking at the bullet wound in his side. His cousin Andy handed him a pint bottle of whiskey and he made Kinnock drink some of it.

"Bullet went clean through, not as bad as it could be," Hodges told Garrity. "I'll get him bandaged and we'll take him back in Mayfield's buckboard. Some of the boys will. I heard what that son of a bitching Klansman said 'bout the plant. What you want to do with Mayfield, the ones that's left?"

"Strip them of their clothes, burn the clothes, then turn them loose, all but Mayfield. Mayfield stays with me."

Hodges got red in the face. "I have four dead and six wounded. Let me kill the Klansmen if you don't want to."

"Turn them loose the way I said," Garrity repeated. "Kinnock, all of you, have to live here after this is over. You don't want the ranch tied to a massacre. Start for town and I'll follow along."

Hodges looked over at Mayfield, still lying with his face pressed to the ground. "I get it," he said.

The Klansmen ran or staggered away as soon as they were stripped. Kinnock's men jeered at them as they went. A few minutes later, Garrity was alone with Mayfield. "Get up, Pig Meat," he said. "On your feet, you rotten, vicious bastard. Judgment Day is here, fat man."

Mayfield had to make several tries before he was able to stand up. He stood there, unsteady on his feet, a quivering mountain of yellowish fat. Naked, he was the most disgusting thing Garrity had ever seen. His mouth moved silently before words finally came out.

"What are you going to do with me?" He slobbered as he spoke. "Can't we make a deal? I'm a rich man. How much money do you want? Say what you want and I'll pay it. Listen, you can turn me over to the Rangers."

"No deal, no Rangers," Garrity said. "Walk down the hill ahead of me. You can't run, you can't get away. Just walk."

They went down the hill and the penned-up javelinas squealed and snorted when the two men got close. Mayfield turned with a bewildered look on his face, as if to say what they were doing didn't make sense. Then Garrity smiled and suddenly Mayfield knew and he screamed and kept on screaming. He stopped screaming when Garrity drew his pistol and drove the wild pigs back by firing in front of them. Mayfield struggled wildly when Garrity unlatched the gate, slashed him with Whittaker's knife and shoved him inside. In an instant, the javelinas were all over him, slashing him with their razor-sharp tusks, driven mad by the smell of blood.

Garrity didn't wait around to see the end of it.

He caught up with the column of riders and followed at slow speed. The buckboard with Kinnock in it was up front to keep the dust from bothering

157

him. Behind the buckboard were the six wounded ranch hands in two wagons. Hodges rode back and Garrity opened the door to talk to him.

"You think we can leave Kinnock and the wounded and ride ahead? We're making no time this way. The boys'll get them home all right."

Garrity nodded and they pulled away, leaving the wounded behind. The road ran straight and flat and Garrity set the Motor Scout moving at top speed, with Hodges and the others galloping behind. After a while, he pulled ahead of them, with the Motor Scout eating up the miles. He was a few miles from town when he saw the column of thick, black smoke rising straight up into the sky. Durkin was in trouble sure enough.

He slowed the Motor Scout until Hodges and his men were behind him again. There was no need to tell Hodges how they would do it. They would do it the same way they had attacked Mayfield's house. Even with the door closed he could hear the heavy firing coming from the direction of the plant. This should finish it, he thought. He hoped it would. He was tired.

He pressed the pedal on the floor, turned the Motor Scout onto the company road that ran down the slope to the plant and the river beyond it. Some of the attackers had pushed wagons together and were firing from behind them. Others were shooting from the cattle pens and the railroad siding. He couldn't see what they were doing on the riverside. They had the plant pinned down tight and there were enough of them to take it if they could set it on fire.

As he sped down the slope, a Klansman jumped to his feet and threw a gasoline-filled bottle with a burning rag for a fuse at the door where Kinnock's office was. The bomb fell short and exploded, covering the ground with a sheet of flame. Garrity opened fire with the machine gun and the men behind the wagons turned and tried to fire back, but he blasted them off their feet with bullets.

Behind him he heard the thunder of hooves and knew Hodges wasn't waiting for the Motor Scout to do most of the killing. Garrity steered the Motor Scout around the wagons, increased speed and roared down toward the cattle pens. The attackers there tried to return fire from behind the rails, but the Motor Scout kept coming, its gun dealing out death.

Garrity stopped the Motor Scout and saturated the cattle pen with bullets until there wasn't a man left alive in it.

He turned the Scout Car and drove back toward the railroad siding, but Hodges's men had already driven the Klansmen out of there and had gone on to deal with the Mayfield men attacking from the riverside of the plant. By the time he got there, they had killed most of the attackers and driven the rest into the muddy river. Some were still in the river, others were climbing the far bank.

Hodges's cowboys poured volley after volley into them and then Garrity drove up close to the riverbank and opened fire with the machine gun. That time there was no stopping Hodges and his men. The river was red with blood. It was their show, as the colonel would say, and he left them to it. He never saw a bunch of men who enjoyed their work more.

He stopped the Motor Scout in front of the office door, but didn't get out until Durkin opened it and came out. He had been creased in the head and his shirt was covered with blood. Some of his men and a lot of plant workers came out after him. He looked at the dead Klansmen lying by the wagons.

"How goes it for law and order?" he said.

"It goes well," Garrity said. "We killed nineteen Klansmen, stripped eleven naked and sent them running, and burned Mayfield's house to the ground."

"And the boss man himself?"

"Mayfield will be seen no more in these parts." Durkin was close enough for Garrity to drop his voice to a whisper. "Don't ask me any more in front of witnesses. I fed the fat bastard to the pigs."

"Good," Durkin said. "I lost three men, no wounded. Two of the cowboys were killed, two wounded. I was beginning to think it was Durkin's Last Stand when they started in with the gasoline bombs. Where's Kinnock?"

"Wounded, on his way back to the ranch. He'll be all right."

Durkin smiled his evil smile. "Tell him his plant's all unionized. I had his people sign up as soon as you left."

At the plant, 27 Klansmen had been killed and 14 wounded. Five had been chased by Hodges's men, roped and dragged back. Garrity ordered them stripped before they were marched through town and turned loose.

With the Klan crushed and humiliated, and Mayfield gone and never to return, the town came back to life, not all at once but gradually. A storekeeper came out and started to sweep the boardwalk in front of his place. A woman walked down the street and went into a store.

Garrity said he was going to look in on the marshal and Durkin said he'd come along. Hodges and about half his men said they'd like to hear what the marshal had to say. The rest of Hodges's men stayed behind to look for Klansmen hiding in the weeds.

But the marshal wasn't there and neither were his deputies. The jail door was open and the desk drawers were pulled out. All the guns were missing from the chained rack and someone had grabbed the coffeepot from the stove. Something glittered at the bottom of the spittoon, and when Durkin kicked it over the marshal's badge clattered to the floor.

"I think the marshal can take a hint," Durkin said. "What say we all have a beer or whatever? Drinks are on the United Workers of America, boys."

The bartender in the Good Times saloon looked ready to run until Durkin grabbed him by his leather necktie and said, "Set 'em, Mac. Billy Whittaker and his boys won't be in today. Billy Whittaker won't be in no time."

Hodges and his men had their drinks and left. Garrity said he'd see them later at the ranch.

"Hey," Durkin said. "That's some automobile you've got. You wouldn't by any chance want to sell it? What I couldn't unionize with a persuader like that."

"Can't do it," Garrity said. "It belongs to the company I work for. Anyway, it won't stand up to artillery fire, maybe not even a Remington Rolling Block."

Durkin tilted his beer bottle. "I wasn't planning to unionize the army, soldier."

"I can't let you have it, and that's final."

"But you will send the Police Model with all the trimmings?"

"I said I would. What are you going to do after this?"

"I plan to stay for a while to make sure his lordship doesn't try to welsh on our deal. Then it's back to Seattle for me. You can send the gun care of Mrs. M.J. Dowd, Front Street, Seattle. Make sure it's insured. There's a lot of thieves in this world. What will you be doing?"

"I have to take the Motor Scout back to New York and report to my boss. You wouldn't like him, Durkin. I don't like him."

Durkin snapped his fingers and the barkeep hurried to uncork another beer. "Ever thought of going into union work? You'd be a natural."

"Too dangerous," Garrity said. "Besides, it doesn't pay enough."

"A pity. We could unionize the whole country together. It's strenuous work, but you'd be doing good for your fellow man."

"Let my fellow man look out for himself. So long, Durkin. You're a bad lad, but you're straight."

"I don't mind that kind of a reference," Durkin said. They shook hands and Garrity went out, got into the Motor Scout, and drove away. Nearly everybody in town came out to look after him. It's done, he thought. Finally it was done.

Kinnock was in bed when he got to the ranch, and one of the men had gone to persuade the old doctor that he didn't have to be afraid of Mayfield anymore. The man with Kinnock went out when Garrity came in.

Garrity sat down on the chair beside the bed. "How are you feeling, my lord?"

His question got a weak smile. "I expect I'll live, your hardship. But I feel bad about the good men who've died. Murdo, Torrance, all of them. Is it really over?"

"It's really over," Garrity said. "With all the killing that's been done, the Rangers will have to come in. I don't see there's much they can do but take sworn statements and write a report. I'll leave my sworn statement with you. I have to get back to New York.

The colonel wouldn't want the Maxim Company to get too mixed up in this."

"I don't suppose you've ever considered becoming a rancher. I have so much land. . . ."

"That's the second offer I've had today. Durkin wants me to unionize mugs and you want me to punch cows. No thanks. I'm not cut out for either. I'll stay a few days, then pack up and leave. The colonel can tell Maxim you're all right. Maxim can tell Queen Victoria."

"I'm done with all that." Kinnock made a sour face. "After all that's happened, this is my home, not because I own my land, but because I fought for it."

"That's the best way to get a feeling for it. Just remember one thing. This trouble will be forgotten and other Mayfields will come along, men who think they're smarter and tougher than he was. Watch out for them."

"I'll do that. You know, I felt like a completely different man when we attacked Mayfield's house. I think I would have killed those Klan prisoners if I'd been able to. Bloody awful thought, isn't it?"

Talking so much made Kinnock cough and Garrity held a glass of water to his lips. "Not so bloody," Garrity said. "The idea is to be tough without getting carried away by it. Be tough when you have to be, other times don't. Don't hang the next poor man you catch stealing a cow is what I mean."

"Odd getting advice from you of all people."

"I guess it is. You better get some rest, Kinnock. I'll be around if you need me."

In the kitchen, Garrity fried up a big steak and drank a bottle of beer. After he'd eaten it and was starting on his report, the elderly doctor came in and the cowhand showed him where Kinnock's room was.

Going on with his report, Garrity wrote about the grenades, and then went on to the Scout Car. He was still writing when the doctor came out and told him Kinnock would be all right.

"I'll be back tomorrow," the doctor said.

Garrity decided to finish his report later; then he drank another beer, went to his room and slept until the next day. After he ate, he drove the Motor Scout into the barn and started to put the huge crate together again. He finished nailing up the Motor Scout and was glad to see the last of it. It was a dandy little automobile, as Durkin called it, but he liked to do his fighting out in the open. He painted over the old stencils and went into the house to look for labels that could be pasted on.

He stayed for two more days, and then it was time to say good-bye to Kinnock. Even then, he couldn't say he liked Kinnock very much. If anything, he had become too confident, a mistake for any man. But he figured that Kinnock, mild mannered or bursting with confidence, would be able to take care of himself from then on.

They shook hands and Garrity was turning to go when Kinnock said, "I know you told me you'd killed Mayfield. Do you mind telling me how you killed him?"

Garrity told him.

"God Almighty!" Kinnock said, but he laughed when he said it, and he was still laughing when Garrity closed the door and went out. The next Mayfield better watch out, Garrity thought.

He was waiting for the spur-line train from Amarillo when it pulled in and two Texas Rangers got off. Both were shortish, wiry men with badges pinned to their shirt pockets. Real hammered-down Southwestern waddies. The depot master wasn't around and one of the Rangers said to Garrity, "Pardon me, mister. You know where the Kinnock packing plant is? They tell me there's been a heap of trouble in this town. Must be some town all right. I never even heard of it."

Garrity told him where they could find the plant. They straightened their shoulders, hitched up their guns, and started for town. They could have stayed on the train for the short ride to the plant siding. But he guessed they wanted to take a look at the town that had seen so much trouble.

Garrity waited for the train to come back, then climbed aboard, and settled in for the long trip to New York.

Chapter Eleven

"You fed him to the what?" the colonel said, raising his bushy eyebrows in astonishment. "Did you say javelins?"

"Javelinas. South Texas wild pigs. Guess it's a Spanish word," Garrity said. "Don't come any wilder. Boars got tusks on them like razors, but they'll kill you quick and then eat you. Mayfield liked to eat them and ended up being et."

Garrity told the colonel about Mayfield's fondness for pig meat. "That fat man would pass up tenderloin for pork chops. Javelina meat is a special taste, but it's pretty good, especially the ham."

"Do you mean you've actually eaten the beastly stuff?"

"Sure. Just the once though. But it's good beastly stuff."

They were in Col. Pritchett's office in the Maxim Company warehouse in New York. Garrity was winding up his report on the destruction of the West Texas Klan, which ended with the death of Pig Meat Mayfield.

"That story of yours is going to put me off my morning bacon for a week," the colonel said. "He that lives by the pig shall die by the pig, eh what!"

Garrity didn't join in the colonel's barking laughter. "I knew you were going to say that," he said.

The colonel's smile turned to a frown. "The trouble with you is you have no sense of humor."

"Sure I have. I fed Mayfield to the pigs, didn't I?"

"I fail to see that as humor. Justice may have been done, but you might as easily have dispatched him with a bullet."

Garrity drank some of the colonel's special Neopolitan blend coffee. It tasted like hot ink. "Too easy," he said. "Pig Meat deserved a lot more than a quick, clean bullet."

"Well he got it, didn't he? What a fearsome fellow you are." Col. Pritchett had been leafing through Garrity's written report. "I'm pleased that you found the grenades so effective. Couldn't have done it without them, eh?"

Garrity decided not to drink any more of the bitter Italian coffee. "I didn't say that. But all right. The grenades were goddamned effective. Not one of them failed to explode and when they blew up arms and legs went flying. The one-pound weight is just right for a long throw."

The colonel looked up from the report. "Any suggestions for improvement?"

"The seven-inch cane handle could be maybe two

or three inches longer. I found it a bit short for throwing. And maybe the cane should be roughened some by painting it with resin for a better grip. As it is it has a slippery feel to it. And don't be telling me my hands were sweaty."

"Mine would be," the colonel lied, making a note of Garrity's suggestion. "Anything else?"

"Tell Maxim he ought to invent a self-exploding grenade with a cast-iron case. No throwing handle. No percussion. Everything inside the cast-iron case. When the case explodes you get a lot more shrapnel. With the present grenade you don't get enough shrapnel and screwing in the detonator takes too much time. I carried the grenades with the detonators already in place."

"You what!" The colonel threw down his pen. "You didn't use the wooden safety plugs until you were ready to arm the grenades?"

"That's right," Garrity said. "But I didn't jump up and down. I was safe enough and the grenades were ready when I needed them. Maybe that saved my life."

The colonel was furious. "You idiot! Why do you think the safety plugs were invented? You don't have to jump up and down to get one of those things to explode. How many did you carry like that at one time?"

"Six. I was able to send them off one right after the other. Nobody was left alive after the last one exploded. Now if I had to hunker down there screwing in detonators. . . ."

The colonel shook his cropped white head. "There's no use talking to you and I'm not going to try. How did you carry these six live grenades? With the throwing handles stuck inside your belt?"

"That's right. But the handles were stuck in tight."

"For Christ's sake, the handles are only seven inches long! Suppose one of them had fallen out and hit the ground hard?"

"Then I wouldn't be here drinking your lousy-tasting coffee. What about my idea for a self-exploder with a cast-iron case? You pull out a pin or turn a short handle, the self-exploder is activated and you have a set amount of time to get rid of it."

"I'm glad you considered that last part," the colonel said. He picked up his pen and talked as he wrote. "As a matter of fact, Mr. Maxim and his staff have been working on a grenade such as you describe in your unscientific way. You are sworn to secrecy, of course. The problem appears to be the self-exploding device. A number have been tested and discarded for one reason or another. One poor staff member is no more, I'm afraid."

Garrity was interested, as he was in all new weapons. "He held on to it too long?"

"No. It exploded as soon as he extracted the safety pin." The colonel grimaced as he wrote. "Of course, it was an experimental grenade and the safety pin should have been pulled by means of a long wire operated from the cover of sandbags. But it was his pet project, so to speak, and he became overconfident. Let that be a lesson to you."

"Next time I'll use a long wire," Garrity said.

"There may not be a next time if you continue to be as reckless as you are. Oh well." The colonel screwed on the cap of his solid gold fountain pen and lay back in his chair. "I see the Motor Scout does not meet with your complete approval. Such a vehicle needs two men, you say."

"One to drive, one to fire the Maxim. It's hard

to steer and fire at the same time. Sure it can be done, but not all that well. Give the gun too much attention and you end up in a ditch. The reverse is equally true. Granted the second man adds weight, but I think it's worth it."

"Are you sure you wouldn't like to go to England to join the staff at the research department? I'm sure Mr. Maxim would be delighted to have you. That way you could find fault with all his inventions without ever leaving the premises."

Garrity pretended to think about his proposal which annoyed the colonel even more. "Well I've never been to England," he said. "A nice little country they tell me. Might be hard to test my weapons though. I hear the English law is pretty strict."

"A real wiseacre, aren't you?" The colonel sneered as only he could. "Well let me tell you something, my good man. Big and hard-bitten as you are, Mr. Maxim would eat you for breakfast."

The colonel continued to glare at Garrity for a good ten seconds. Then he said quietly, "You're right about the Motor Scout, of course, and I will include your comments in my own report. We're not paying you to be an arsekisser, are we? I'm sure Mr. Maxim would be the first to agree."

"Good old Hiram," Garrity said. "Tell him Two-Gun Kinnock says howdy."

Col. Pritchett put Garrity's report in a drawer. It would be sent to Hiram Maxim after it was put into the secret company code. Trusting no one on his office staff, the colonel did all the coding himself.

"How did you leave Kinnock?" the colonel asked. There was nothing about Kinnock in Garrity's report.

"Thinking straighter than when I met him," Garrity said. "I doubt if he'll need any outside help from here on in. Mayfield is in pig heaven and the Klansmen have put the sheets back on the bed, so that part is done with. But he'll have more trouble along the way. A man with that much land always does. Somebody is always trying to take it away from him. Soon he'll be making big money and they'll try to grab that too. If not real crooks, then the meat packers in the Midwest. Christ knows what they'll do to drive him out of business."

Col. Pritchett's one good eye bored into Garrity like a gimlet. "Get to the fucking point."

"Whatever they—whoever they are—throw at him I think he'll be able to handle it because he's learned that everybody in the world is a selfish son of a bitch no matter what he says to make you think he isn't. I'm a son of a bitch for my Zunis. You're a son of a bitch for money."

"I beg your pardon, sir," the colonel said stiffly.

"No offense meant, Colonel. You asked me about Kinnock and I'm telling you. Kinnock started out wanting to do good for his fellow man. Anyway that's what he thought though I doubt he knew the real reason. He still may not know but at least he's stopped his mealymouthed bullshit. He won't go back to it because it will sound tinhorn even to himself. Things are a lot more simple for him after what he's been through. Next time some bastard tries to make trouble for him he won't wring his hands about what to do about it. What's more, I think he'll enjoy it."

"And that's your point?"

"That's my point. I think there was a mean son of

a bitch hiding back there all the time. The Klan gave Kinnock an excuse to finally let him loose and now he's a better man for it."

"Amazing! I send you to Texas on a job and you come back spouting stuff about Kinnock's mental state. You should get together with that quack over in Vienna I've been reading about in the *Times*. Bloody charlatan claims all our troubles are in our heads."

"Where do you think they are?"

"In our crotches. That's where all the trouble in the world stems from."

"Why is it," Garrity asked, changing the subject, "that when you sent me to Texas there was good cold ale and now there's nothing?"

The colonel swung his pipe reamer, another of his many mannerisms. "It's because I was so delighted to hear you were safe and sound that I forgot to order the ale."

"You wouldn't want to order it now? I'm in no hurry."

"Always trying to put one over on me, aren't you? In point of fact, I'm much too busy to sit here while you sit there guzzling. But I'm in a generous mood today and you did do a fine job in Texas, even if you told Kinnock he didn't have to pay for the rifles he ordered through you. So I'll tell you what I'll do. Take a cab to McSorley's, eat and drink as much as you like, and tell them to send the bill to me."

Garrity stood up and put on his hat. "I tried that on my own bat last time I was in town. Young McSorley absolutely refused to extend credit to any bloody Englishman. I was out nearly thirty dollars. You wouldn't want to settle that out of petty cash?"

172

"Sue me," the colonel said.

Garrity waved and went down the steel stairs three at a time. He'd have to run like hell to catch the next train west.

CHEYENNE

JUDD COLE

Born Indian, raised white, Touch the Sky swears he'll die a free man. Don't miss one exciting adventure as the young brave searches for a world he can call his own.

#1: Arrow Keeper.
__3312-7 $3.50 US/$4.50 CAN

#2: Death Chant.
__3337-2 $3.50 US/$4.50 CAN

#3: Renegade Justice.
__3385-2 $3.50 US/$4.50 CAN

#4: Vision Quest.
__3411-5 $3.50 US/$4.50 CAN

LEISURE BOOKS
ATTN: Order Department
276 5th Avenue, New York, NY 10001

Please add $1.50 for shipping and handling for the first book and $.35 for each book thereafter. PA., N.Y.S. and N.Y.C. residents, please add appropriate sales tax. No cash, stamps, or C.O.D.s. All orders shipped within 6 weeks via postal service book rate. Canadian orders require $2.00 extra postage and must be paid in U.S. dollars through a U.S. banking facility.

Name_____

Address_____

City _____ State _____ Zip _____

I have enclosed $_____in payment for the checked book(s).
Payment <u>must</u> accompany all orders.☐ Please send a free catalog.

WILDERNESS

GIANT SPECIAL EDITION:
SEASON
OF THE WARRIOR

By David Thompson

*Tough mountain men, proud Indians, and an America
that was wild and free—authentic frontier adventure
during America's Black Powder Days.*

The savage, unmapped territory west of the Mississippi
presents constant challenges to anyone who dares to venture
into it. And when a group of English travelers journey into
the Rockies, they have no defense against the fierce Indians,
deadly beasts, and hostile elements. If Nate and his friend
Shakespeare McNair can't save them, the young adventurers
will suffer unimaginable pain before facing certain death.
_3449-2 $4.50 US/$5.50 CAN